THE PROMISE

EMILY SHINER

INKUBATOR
BOOKS

Published by Inkubator Books
www.inkubatorbooks.com

ISBN (eBook): 978-1-915275-11-0
ISBN (Paperback): 978-1-915275-10-3
ISBN (Hardback): 978-1-915275-12-7

PROLOGUE
SCOTT

"The court finds the defendant not guilty." The judge manages to maintain his composure while he reads the verdict, but I hear the note of disbelief in his voice. My heart pounds hard, and I stare at him like I want to make sure that he's serious and isn't going to suddenly change his mind.

The entire courtroom seems to be frozen. I glance over at the jury, who are all doing their best to keep their faces stony and still. It's obvious that they don't want to look at anyone, don't want to acknowledge what they just did.

"Well done, Scott," the man next to me whispers. His voice is low so that nobody will be able to hear what he just said. The reporters relegated to the back of the courtroom don't stand a chance of hearing his words, and there are very few people in the actual room to watch the trial.

That's on me. I did everything I could to keep this trial out of the papers, knowing full well that the news would eat it up.

Doctor Charged with Medical Malpractice after Death During Routine Surgery.

There's no way that I would have been able to get any

sympathy from the jury if that sort of headline were all over the papers. We managed to keep it so hush-hush that even my wife doesn't know what kind of case I'm working on. She's aware that I was planning on being late every night this week, but she doesn't need to know the gritty details.

"Doctor, you're free to go." I turn to my client and eyeball him, trying to decide whether I did the right thing. Sure, I've helped a lot of people avoid time behind bars, some of them worse than the man standing in front of me. At the same time, there are definitely people who won't ever see the light of day again who deserve to be free when compared with this man.

I know the truth about what he did. It wasn't just medical malpractice, although that's what we managed to call it. If it were, that would mean that he'd made a mistake or two and the patient on the table died under his care.

They died, but it's not because he made a mistake.

This man knew exactly what he was doing the entire time he was setting up illicit organ donations. I can only imagine the absolute zoo parade that the courthouse would be if anyone knew the truth, that he was harvesting organs from patients during routine surgeries and then transplanting them into rich patients who offered ridiculous sums of money.

Thank goodness for him that I wanted to keep my mouth shut and earn my fee or he wouldn't ever see the light of day again.

But it's not because I'm nice. That's not why I worked so hard to make sure that he would be free from the charges against him.

No, I worked so hard because I have a very personal motivation to see him out of jail.

"I'd better get out of here before the angry mob comes

after me." He flashes me a huge grin and then turns to leave the courtroom.

I should follow him, should escort him out past anyone who might want to stop him and talk to him.

Taking a deep breath, I force my feet to move so that I can go after him. I know that my presence isn't going to stop the angry whispers from family members, but I should be able to keep people from actually coming up to him or attacking him.

Their anger is not my problem. I came here to do a job, and I did it. I did it so well that the doctor is free to practice medicine again. Sure, he lost his rights at the local hospital, but really, that's barely a slap on the wrist compared to what he did.

We hurry through the courthouse and walk outside. The cool afternoon air is a little damp, and I turn to say goodbye to him, fully intending to get back inside as soon as possible. I want to check in on my wife and make sure that she's okay. I haven't had time to check in on her all day long, not with today being the final day of the trial.

"You were a good lawyer," the doctor says, turning and grabbing my hand. He gives me a firm handshake, looking me right in the eyes. "I'm still not entirely sure how you did it, but I appreciate all you did for me. You know that you can give me a call if I can ever return the favor."

I'm at a loss for words right now. Honestly, even when I took the case, I wasn't confident that I'd be able to get him free and clear of all charges. "You kept your mouth shut at the right times," I tell him, which is the only thing I asked him to do. "Enjoy the rest of your life and try to stay out of trouble. I don't think we can pull this off again."

He laughs, the sound sudden and sharp in the silence. "Oh, I'm sure that the two of us could do whatever we wanted. Do let me know if you ever need my services."

My stomach sinks. I know whom I kept out of jail. I know that my wife would be horrified if she knew the kind of person I'd just helped. She'd be even more horrified if she knew that I was actually thinking of taking him up on his offer.

Not yet. The buzz surrounding him needs to die down. I need to make sure that I'm right about how sick my wife is. There's no reason to jump the gun on this, not when I'm pretty sure that we have a little while longer. Long enough to do some more tests, to make sure that I'm doing the right thing.

The doctor turns away from me, but I call out, stopping him in his tracks. "Your business card," I say. "I might need it."

He grins, the sight of his smile making my stomach twist, then pulls a small piece of paper from his pocket. "No business cards, but you can have my personal cell." He presses the scrap into my hand, and I shove it deep into my pocket as I watch him walk away.

When he disappears from sight, I pull my phone out and tap on the screen. It's time to check in on my wife and make sure that things are going well for her. I don't like not being able to keep an eye on her throughout the day.

She doesn't have any idea of just how devoted I really am.

1

Sunday drives are supposed to be lazy. They're the perfect time for exploring a new place or just driving around with someone you love, but as I pull off the main road that leads out of town and drive past the last gas station, I feel my heart start to pick up the pace.

This drive isn't lazy, and it certainly isn't a joyride. My wife, Erin, sits next to me, humming along mindlessly to the music on the radio, and I keep my eyes focused on the road ahead so that I don't miss the one thing that I'm looking for.

"Would you look at that?" I keep my voice light and lift one hand from the steering wheel to point at a billboard set up over the marshy land that developers want to put a mall on. They can't, not without disturbing the various plants and animals that live there, and there's often a group of nature lovers stationed there with signs and chants to drive people away from even considering it.

"Look at what?" Erin turns in the direction I'm pointing and sucks in a gasp. "'Please help, looking for a live kidney donor.' You've got to be kidding me, Scott. Who in the world has to put a request for a kidney on a billboard? That's terrible."

"You'd be surprised." We zip past the billboard, and I feel myself relax. "Seriously, Erin, the wait list for a kidney is ridiculous. People die every year while they wait to be selected to get one, and a lot of people turn to asking their friends and family members for a kidney."

"I can see that, but putting up a billboard outside of town?" She shakes her head and reaches out, turning down the radio so that we can talk a little better. "Can you imagine how scary that must be?"

"I heard that she got one," I say, turning onto a small road that will wind through the mountains and finally spit us back out on our side of town. Now that we've driven by the billboard, I don't really care to continue our drive. There are always things to do at the house, and I know that Erin has a massive pile of laundry waiting on her when we get back. "A kidney. She's one of the lucky ones. She probably just has to wait for the lease on the billboard to run out before it will get replaced."

"It's terrible." She reaches over and squeezes my arm. "I can't imagine how scary that would be to have to go through, you know? Asking some stranger to take pity on you and give you an organ?" She shudders, and I can't help but reach out and pat her knee.

My Erin is perfect. She's so sweet, so kind, and so fragile. Ever since the moment I met her, I knew that I would do whatever it took to keep her safe. That's why I wanted to take this drive, not just to show off the billboard, but so that I could say the next thing on my mind.

"You know, some of the guys at work were talking about donations and what goes into them. I guess the fact that this billboard worked has inspired someone else to start looking for help. Sounds like she's working with a doctor to try to find a match instead of going on the registry."

"Really? Do you think it's going to become pretty common to do that?"

I shrug, letting the stress of the conversation roll off my back. As sweet as my Erin is, she's also that easy to control. I'm sure that I'll have her coming around to my way of thinking in a few minutes.

"I don't know, but apparently, this is a single mom, and she's running out of time. She works all the time to take care of her daughter, but I have no idea how much longer she'll be able to work as she continues to get sicker. I don't know what she'll do if she doesn't get a kidney, but it doesn't sound good."

"That's terrible." Erin's voice is full of sadness, and I risk a glance over at her. "Do you think someone will step up to help her?"

"Hard to say." We stop at a red light, and I reach over to take her hand, linking our fingers together. "Honey, I'm sorry. I didn't mean to upset you. I just thought that this was interesting, that you'd want to know what's going on."

"No, you didn't do anything wrong." The words spill out of her, and she shakes her head firmly. "I'm fine, really, Scott. It's just so sad, and it makes me wish that I could help her. Do you know what blood type she is?"

I do. Of course I do. Dr. Thomas told me everything I need to know about this woman, everything that I need to tell Erin to get her on board with the donation. She's so innocent and trusting that I'd always do the right thing for her that it never once crosses her mind that she needs to question what she's being told.

"I think I wrote it down on a scrap of paper," I tell her. "It's probably still in my pants from Friday, come to think of it.

You know that I always forget to empty them out before you run the wash."

This makes her laugh, and the tension in the car instantly disappears. "Do I ever! I think you're just preparing me for the day we finally have kids, Scott." Her fingers tighten on mine, and I know what she's going to ask me. "Do you think that now's a good time to talk about starting a family? You're doing great at work. You're moving up all the time. We don't have to worry about money, and we bought this amazing house so that we could have kids. It just seems silly not to fill the house with laughter and little feet, don't you think?"

I actually feel my heart squeeze in response to my wife's words. All she's wanted from the day we met was to have a family, but I keep putting it off. First, I wanted to make sure that we had the right house for little kids. I wanted a big backyard and a safe neighborhood where they could ride their bikes.

Next, I wanted to make sure that I was in a good, steady job. The last thing I wanted was to switch up my career when we had little kids underfoot. I know how disruptive that can be for a family, and I refuse to do it to mine.

Finally, I have to make sure that Erin is healthy. If she's going to be the mother of my children, then I need to be absolutely sure that nothing is going to happen to her. I have to be sure that she'll be able to keep up with them while they're little and that she'll be able to get down on the floor with them and play.

I remember my own mother being so sick that she would spend most of the time stretched out on the sofa, unable to play with me. No kid wants to play by themselves all the time. I want Erin running around outside, making cookies with our kids, and curling up in forts with them. She can't do that if she's sick.

"I think we're closer to having that discussion than we've

ever been," I finally tell her, and she sighs in happiness. "I know that you have an appointment tomorrow with the doctor, so let's see how it goes, okay?"

"Okay! Oh, Scott, you have no idea how happy this makes me. Having a family with you . . . it's everything. That's all I want." Her face darkens a little bit, and I know without asking that she's thinking about the woman I told her about who needs a kidney to survive.

I don't bring it up again, though.

I don't need to.

If there's one thing I know about my wife, it's how to make her do exactly what I want her to.

2

ERIN

It takes until Friday before I finally make an appointment to see the doctor, and I'm thrilled when I get in the same day. The paper gown I'm in crinkles as I shift on the examination table. It's chilly in here, and I rub my hands up and down my arms to try to combat the goosebumps growing there. I swear, I was just in for a physical. Scott really wanted me to see Dr. Thomas, a new doctor who just moved to the area a few years ago. I've been seeing him for a year, but I can't help the fact that I'm still nervous going in to visit with him.

He's incredibly focused and passionate about what he does. Even though he can come across as a little intense, I trust him because I know that Scott wouldn't ever put me in a position where I wasn't getting the best care. He's always adamant that I take care of myself, from telling me to spring for the more expensive organic groceries to making sure that I have a pass to the gym and to the local yoga studio.

Of course, since he works every day and I don't, I get to visit them all the time. I'm in the best shape of my life, and that must be why Scott is finally willing to talk about having kids with me. I don't care what hoops I have to jump through to make it happen. I want my own children.

But at the same time, I can't get this woman who needs a kidney donation out of my head. When Scott told me that she's a single mom, I swear that I felt my heart break. Here I am, wanting kids more than anything in the world, and there's a woman who has one but might not be around to take care of her.

How selfish am I that the thought of donating a kidney to her scares me? But at the same time, I want to learn more about it. Glancing over at my purse, I wish that I had another moment to get up and make sure that the scrap of paper I took from Scott's pants last night is still in there, but I'm sure it is.

It not only has the woman's blood type scrawled on it in his hurried handwriting, but also the woman's first name.

I kick my legs, trying to warm up, when the door finally opens and Dr. Thomas strolls in. He gives me a grin and puts down his laptop before walking right over to me to shake my hand.

"Erin," he says, his voice filling the small room, "it's so good to see you again! You're looking just as healthy as a horse today."

I grin at him, unsure of what to say. "Thank you. How does my blood work look?"

"Amazing." He sits down on the spinning stool across the room from me and opens his laptop, tapping at it for a moment. "It all looks good. I'll get the results sent over to you and Scott right away."

"Can I see them?" I've never asked this question before. It doesn't matter how many appointments I've had, I've never once asked to see the results of my tests. It feels strange to say it, but since Scott always takes care of everything, it's never been a problem. Today, though, I want to see them. I want to know how healthy I am.

Not only to have children, which is my dream goal, but also to talk about this woman who needs a kidney. It's probably a harebrained idea, but I can't get it out of my mind. After finding her name in Scott's pocket, I went online to try to find her, but I couldn't find her social media. I wish that I could find her online, but there are tons of reasons someone might not be active on social media.

Maybe she doesn't have social media because she doesn't want people to know how sick she is. Or maybe she's off it so that she can make sure she's protecting her daughter.

The thought of a daughter watching her mom get sicker and sicker makes me feel ill.

How can I even think about having kids right now when someone might die and leave their child an orphan?

"You don't need to worry about anything, Erin," he tells me, closing his laptop and smiling at me. "Believe me, you're healthy. You're in amazing shape, and you do everything that you can to take care of yourself." He pauses, his eyes focused on my face. "But it seems to me like there's something you want to talk about. Something bothering you?"

Yes. No. I take a deep breath, trying to figure out how to broach this conversation with him. It's not that I'm afraid to talk to him, it's just that it seems like a strange conversation to have.

"Do you think I'd be a good option for a kidney donor?" The words spill out of me like water flowing from a dam, and I twist my fingers together in my lap, avoiding looking at him until the silence between us grows so thick that I force myself to glance up at him.

"That's an incredibly selfless thing to ask," he tells me.

"But looking at your tests, yes. I can't imagine that there are many people in this world who would be a better option to be a donor. What brought this on?"

There's something about him that makes me feel safe, like I can tell him everything without worrying about his judging me, so I do, the words coming faster and faster. I tell him about the billboard, about how Scott mentioned the woman he heard about from work. I tell him that I looked up kidney donations last night online and learned about the long wait times.

I don't tell him that I know the woman's name.

"I don't know if I'm being crazy," I tell him, "or if this is something that I really want to do, but I needed to talk to someone about it. I just . . . Dr. Thomas, I want kids. I want a house full of them. But what kind of person would I be to bring more kids into this world when there's one already here who might lose her mom if someone doesn't help her? I could be that person, I know I could."

"You're willing to give up a kidney to someone you don't know?" Before I can answer, he continues, "I think that's one of the most amazing things I've ever heard, Erin. And you say that you're the same blood type?"

I nod, my heart slamming. I'm so glad that I asked him this. I don't know how it's going to pan out, but I want to see it through.

"First things first—you need to talk to Scott about it. I can't encourage you to go down this path if you don't have him completely on board with you. It'll require tests and workups beforehand to make sure that you two are a good match. Then there is some aftercare required, so Scott will have to be on the same page."

"He will be," I say. "Even though I haven't talked to my husband about this, I still honestly believe that he'll want me to go down this path. He'll support me, I'm sure of it." Even as I say the words, I hope that I'm right. Scott loves me and will do anything he can to support me, but what if he thinks I'm putting myself at risk? Then I'm sure he won't back me.

"Then I commend you for thinking of other people before you think of your own needs," he says with a nod. "There aren't many people in this world who would. Most people constantly try to get ahead themselves. It takes a special person to be a donor. If you're willing to go through it, then I can't think of a better gift that you can give someone. Do you have any questions you want to ask me about the process?"

I shake my head. I did a lot of reading last night, going so far as to sit on the toilet at two in the morning scrolling through articles on my phone. I researched kidney transplants, but I want to know more about this woman. *Kathleen.* Scott gave me as much information as he had, including where she works part-time, but he didn't know much more than that. Some of his co-workers know her and told him that she's amazing. They also told him she's running on borrowed time.

I know she's a single mom with one daughter, she needs a kidney, and that she works at a bar called the Angry Donkey. I didn't think it was enough for me to go on, but I found her. I found the woman I want to donate my kidney to. She was right there on my computer screen, smiling at the camera with the rest of the bartenders. She looked tired in the photo. I had gasped, then committed her face to memory.

I want to make sure that I'm doing the right thing by putting my dreams of having a family on hold. If she's really such a good mom and so in need of my help, then I can't look the other way when I know that she needs someone to save her. That's just not who I am, and I refuse to be changed by the fact that Scott might finally be ready to have a family.

No, the best thing for me to do is talk to him about this. I also want to get closer to Kathleen and make sure that she's as amazing as my husband says she is. If I'm going to put my dreams on hold one more time, then I want to make sure that I'm doing this for the right person.

3

ERIN

"I think that it's an incredible idea." Scott eyeballs me from across the small café table where we're grabbing a cup of coffee. It's been a week since we took our drive last Sunday and he drove me past the billboard asking for a kidney donation. One week, and the scrap of paper I took from his pocket is all I've been able to think about.

Right now, he's watching me like he's never seen me before. There's love in his eyes, and I want to reach out and take his hand to pull him to me, but we got a high-top table in the corner of the café, and I can't touch him without stretching all the way across the table.

Around us, other customers laugh and eat, downing huge lattes and Danishes the size of your face, totally unaware that at our table, I'm trying to save someone's life, and my husband is one hundred percent behind me.

"I had a feeling you would say that. I'm so glad you agree." Pushing my latte out of the way, I plant my elbows on the table so that I can lean forward and get a better look at my husband. He's getting older—we both are—but that doesn't mean I'm any less attracted to him. The touch of gray around his temples makes him look distinguished, but he still takes care of his body just as well as I take care of myself.

"Erin, I can't believe you're so willing to do it. You have the most beautiful heart out of anyone I've ever met. That's why I fell in love with you." He reaches out to take my hands, and I lean forward to meet him halfway.

Is the edge of the table cutting into my stomach? Sure is.

Do I care? Not right now.

"As long as you think it's a good idea. It's just something I haven't been able to stop thinking about since you mentioned it. And then, at my appointment with Dr. Thomas, he said that I seemed like a good candidate for a donor. You know I love to help people."

"Usually just by baking them casseroles when they're having a hard time and making sure that you pick up trash at the park," he says with a laugh. "Donating a kidney to a complete stranger doesn't really fall under the umbrella of *normal helping*. I hope you realize just how incredible that makes you."

I wave away his praise. "If I don't help her, then who will? I just . . . wow. I can't get this out of my head. Seriously, Scott, what if that were me up there? What if I were the one needing a kidney and someone had one that they could give me and they wouldn't do it because it went *above and beyond* the level of giving that society tells them is appropriate?"

Bingo. All of my cards are on the table right now. I've made it clear to Scott just how important this is to me, and now the ball is in his corner. He knows that I'll defer to him, of course, but I really want to do this. I want him to support me while I save someone's life.

And he's going to. That's just who he is, always supporting me, always looking out for me. I can't imagine him trying to change my mind about this when he knows how important it is to me.

Just the thought of donating my kidney gives me goosebumps. It's not every day that you get to give someone the gift of life without actually giving birth to them.

Scott's watching me like he can read my mind, and I'm sure he can. So far, he hasn't argued with me. He's been supportive, but I want to make sure to really drive the point home that I want to do this.

In fact, I guess it's good that he's not being overly supportive or pushing me to do this. Scott always wants what's best for me, so he just has to see that this is what I think is the best option for me to do right now.

What if I'd been in that terrible accident before we got married and a Good Samaritan hadn't stopped and pulled me from the car before it burst into flames? I'd hardly be sitting across from him right now at our favorite café if someone hadn't gone out of their way to make sure that I wouldn't die.

"Don't bring up the accident," he tells me, pointing a finger at me before draining the last of his coffee. "I'm serious, Erin, you don't need to do that to convince me, okay? I'm on your team here, and if this is something that you really want to do, then you have me behind you all the way. I'm always on your side, have been from the day I met you. We just have to do everything possible to keep you safe, okay? You just have to make sure that you're a match. You might have to undergo hormone treatments beforehand, I don't know. It's a major surgery, and we both need to make sure that we're on the same page."

I feel a flush of excitement wash over me. "Thank you." Leaning across the table, I take his hand. "You're always so supportive of what I want to do, Scott. I couldn't do this without you."

Scott wants nothing more than to keep me safe and healthy, but he also knows how important this is to me. I can be healthy and save someone's life, and he sees that. How did I get so lucky?

Like he said, baking someone a casserole is one thing, but donating a kidney to them is something else entirely. Even though I know this is risky, he's got my back like he always does.

"I will. Of course I will, Erin." Leaning back in his chair, he crosses his arms on his chest.

It's his power move, the one that I'm sure he uses in the courtroom all the time to get people to shut up and pay attention to him. I've been smitten with him ever since I saw him do that the first time.

He might be a terror in the courtroom, but he's never been anything but kind with me. Nobody wants what's best for me more than Scott does. That's probably why he pushes me to take such good care of myself and why he's always talking to my doctor to ensure that I'm healthy. His love for me is why our marriage works so well. We're honest with each other about what we want and what we fear, and it's that honesty that makes us so strong.

That's why I'm talking to him about this right now, even though I feel like I already made up my mind. There wasn't any way that I could go behind his back on this one. I need Scott's support, and I have it.

"You want to do this?"

I nod.

He grins at me. "Then you need to know that I'm so proud of you. To even consider helping someone like this is incredible and is a real testament to how incredible you are."

"Thank you." The words almost get caught in my throat, I'm so worked up right now.

Scott nods. "We need to talk to your doctor. It's important that they say that you're the best possible match so things don't go wrong for the recipient, okay? And I want to know that you're as healthy as possible before we pursue this."

"Deal." I'm grinning like a fool, but I can't wipe the smile off my face. My entire life, I've wanted to take care of someone, to give someone life. I always thought that it would be my own kids first, but maybe I was wrong. Maybe this is how I'm going to give someone life.

It might not be traditional, but that's okay. It takes a special person, like Dr. Thomas told me, and I think I'm that person. Then, when I know that this Kathleen is healthy and will be able to take care of her daughter, Scott and I can start our own family.

Looking across the table at my husband, I realize just how in love with him I am. He's so supportive and caring. Even when he works long hours, he's always got time for me, especially on the weekends when he can put everything aside and focus on the two of us.

It has to be exhausting, managing his law firm and making sure that the paralegals are always doing what they're supposed to. Sure, he has staff to handle that, but I know my husband. He prefers to be hands-on and make sure that he's always involved in whatever's happening.

Any little moving piece, and Scott is there.

That's why I knew that I had to come to him about this first. He's my partner, and I know I can't do this without him.

"Thank you," I say, reaching out and grabbing one of his hands to squeeze it. "You have no idea how important this is to me. Imagine giving someone life like this! Nobody else is stepping up, and I want to be the one to do it. I have to help her, and knowing that you support me is . . . well, it's amazing."

"You're a better person than I am." His eyes are locked on mine, and I smile at him. "Seriously, Erin, I've driven by that billboard a dozen times going out of town and never once thought about whether I'd even consider donating a kidney to someone. To family, sure, but not to a stranger. You're a good person for even considering it."

4

SCOTT

It's been two days since Erin approached me at the café about donating her kidney to someone she doesn't even know. I've been watching her as much as possible since then, trying to get a bead on whether she's going forward with the plans or if she's really taking time to think about it before she makes up her mind.

I love my wife. I love how kind she is, how caring. I love that she would willingly give her shirt off her back to a stranger if they needed something to wear. She'd open up our house to anyone who needed a hot meal and a place to stay and is more than willing to open up our checkbook when charities come knocking.

I knew that she would want to help and that I could convince her it was the right thing to do. There are tons of people in the world offering lip service and saying they'll go out on a limb for strangers, but to actually do it is something else entirely. Erin's the type to help anyone, especially with my telling her what a good idea it is.

I also knew that she was going to go digging to get more information about Kathleen. There wasn't any way that she would be able to stand not knowing more about her, especially when I had put the bug in her brain about helping.

Sure, I could just tell her that this is something that needs to happen, but I want to protect Erin. It's best if she comes to that decision on her own. She's so fragile, so small and sweet, that I never want to come clean with her about the fact that she's actually the one who's sick.

It would kill her. After so many years of working out and eating healthy, if she knew that the doctor told me there was a problem with one of her kidneys, she'd be devastated. I know her, and I know that she wouldn't ever want to take the chance to live from someone else.

That's why I have to be the one to do it. I have to be the one willing to make things happen to keep Erin safe. Sure, the doctor said that there was only a small possibility of her kidney failing in the next ten years, but that's too much of a possibility for me to live with.

I had a sick mom. I know how terrible it is. I know that it can ruin your childhood, and I'm not letting it happen to any kids Erin and I have. She's got to be perfect and healthy in order to be the best mom that she can be, and I'm willing to do whatever it takes to make sure that she is.

That's where she and I are different. I love my wife more than I've ever loved anything in my life. But where she's willing to put her needs aside so that someone else can be happy, I'm not. I'm never going to put anyone ahead of her, no matter what it takes.

So if the only way to make sure she gets a kidney is to lie to her and make her think that she's actually the donor, I'll do that. I'll do whatever it takes to save my wife's life.

So far, Erin hasn't questioned the things I've done to improve her life. She loves the healthy food I have her buy, loves that she gets to work out and do yoga whenever she wants. Of course, she's not always thrilled with the multiple doctor appointments I have her go to, but she hasn't questioned me once because she knows that I'm only doing what's best for her.

Sure, every once in a while, she asks to see her reports from the doctor, but those are for my eyes only. I have her go for regular tests so I can make sure that she's healthy.

If she's not healthy, we can't have kids. She wants kids, wants them more than anything. I'll give them to her. I'll give her a house full of children if that's what she wants and if that will make her happy. I love that I've been able to provide for her and give her exactly what she needs. It's fun to take care of her because she's always so thankful.

"Are you in the courtroom or in the office today?" Erin asks, pulling me from my thoughts while she puts a plate with toast and scrambled eggs down in front of me. While she waits for me to respond, she sits down in the chair across from me and rests her chin in her hand. We have an eat-in kitchen, which will be great once we have children, but right now, the house feels overwhelmingly large.

Spearing a bite of eggs, I chew them while I think. "I'll swing by the courtroom this morning, but my next case doesn't actually start until tomorrow, so I'll be in the office most of the day. Why? You baking cookies and bringing them by or something? Last time you did that, Marianne said she needed a warning before you came so that she could take the day off. She's trying to lose weight for her wedding and ended up eating a dozen cookies."

This makes Erin laugh, and she lightly touches her throat as she does so. Her huge diamond ring sparkles in the overhead lighting, throwing tiny rainbows around the kitchen.

"No, nothing like that. I was just going to run some errands and hit the yoga studio. Nothing too taxing today." She grins at me like she just told me that she'd won the lottery or something, but I know she's not telling me the truth.

She's going to hunt down Kathleen, the woman who needs a kidney. I know this because I know exactly what she's been doing on her phone when she thinks she's so sneaky. I know that she's been trying to find Kathleen on social media and probably wants to get closer to her to see what kind of person she really is. I also know that she's looked up the bar where Kathleen works and that she's going to be tempted to check the woman out. The Angry Donkey has a ridiculously comprehensive website, and I was surprised to see Kathleen in a photo of all the bartenders. The photo is labeled, and I'm sure that Erin now knows exactly what she looks like.

"Sounds like a fun day. You still taking that hot yoga that kicked your butt that one time?"

Erin flaps her hand at me like my words are mosquitos and she's waving them away. "It wasn't that bad. And no, I'm not. But I think I'll try it again sometime. Maybe on Saturday, if you want to go sweat with me."

"Not a chance. You'd have better luck getting me to the opera than to hot yoga. I'm pretty sure there's a lawsuit there waiting to happen."

"Not everything demands a lawsuit," she tells me. "You've just got work on the brain." She pauses, chewing on her lower lip, and I know she's thinking about Kathleen. She has to be, since the woman fills up her search history. My little spy app on her phone makes it easy for me to see exactly what she's doing on her phone. The question is whether she's going to mention her to me.

I can wait. I know my wife, and I know that she's going to go through with this. If she loses steam or gets scared, then I know exactly what to say to encourage her again.

"I've been thinking about the kidney donation," she finally says. "I think I want to meet her."

"Kathleen?" I try to act surprised. "What's the rush?"

"She needs help, and I can help her. Can you imagine if I didn't step up and something terrible were to happen to her?" Erin pins me in place with a stare so serious that she looks carved out of marble for a moment. "What would I do then?"

"I get that you want to help her," I say, knowing full well that I need to be very careful choosing my words right now. I need to be supportive, but I can't come across like I'm over the moon about her donating her kidney. If I seem balanced and thoughtful, then she'll believe me when I push her to do the right thing. "I really want you to be careful, Erin. I don't know what I'd ever do if something were to happen to you. But if you want to meet her, then I think it's not a bad idea. Talk things out, get to know each other. That'll help you feel better about making the decision."

Erin nods and pushes back from the table, walking over to the coffeepot to pour herself a cup. I'm pretty sure her hands are shaking a little bit, but when she grips the mug with both hands, I think that maybe I imagined it.

"You know that I support you one hundred percent." I push back from the table and go to her, wrapping my arms around her and pulling her to my chest. "I just love you so much, Erin. I have to make sure that you're safe."

She visibly relaxes. "I know, Scott, and that's something I love about you, but you don't need to worry about me. I know what I'm doing. I feel like . . ." She sighs and gives a shrug. "I feel like I'm being called to do this."

There it is. There's my sweet Erin who will do whatever it takes to help someone else out.

"And that's why you're the most amazing woman I know."

She pulls back from me, and I swear that her eyes are shining a little bit with excitement. "You have no idea, Scott, just how much I want to do this. It's the right thing, I promise you. You'll see."

I knew she would take the bait. Erin has always been good and kind, and even though giving an organ to a stranger goes above and beyond what I expect someone to be willing to do, I knew she would want to help Kathleen.

Last summer, she opened up our backyard for a charity dinner that raised money for local homeless. To really drive home the point about what kind of conditions some people lived in, she'd even set up a few tents in the front yard so that neighbors would feel really blessed in their homes and give her plenty of money for the charity.

It worked and was apparently the most lucrative dinner the organization had ever held. When they wanted to hold it here again this summer, the neighbors offered to double the amount they'd donated just to keep the tents out of the yard, but that didn't stop her.

Erin always does what she can to help people. If I told her that she needed a transplant, she would have fought me tooth and nail. But because she thinks she's helping someone else, she's going to want to do this. I know it.

"I know it's the right thing," I tell her, kissing her on the forehead. "I'm not arguing with you about that. Hell, Erin, I'm not arguing with you at all. I think that this is an incredible gift you want to give Kathleen, and by doing so, you can really change her life."

And yours.

5

My hands tremble as I pull my keys from the ignition and drop them into my purse. Closing my eyes, I take three deep breaths, then open them again and stare at the small bar on the end of Main Street.

I don't drink a lot, mostly a glass of wine at dinner with Scott, but only one. The last thing I want is to feel terrible in the morning when I hit the gym. While wine tastes amazing, it's not the best option for hydrating after a workout. Eyeballing the bar, I doubt whether they'll even serve wine in here or if I'll have to order something stronger. I don't even remember the last time I was in a bar, but this is where Kathleen works, and I want to see her in person before I reach out to her.

Scott has no idea that I'm here. He thinks I'm at my morning barre workout, which is where I usually am on Mondays right before lunch, but I skipped it to come here instead. My instructor has called twice and texted once to make sure that I'm okay since I never miss, so I shoot her a quick text letting her know that I'm totally fine before I get out of the car and walk to the Angry Donkey.

It's dark inside, and I have to let my eyes adjust a little after the heavy door swings shut behind me. As soon as I can see a bit better, I let my eyes skim around the room. The bar is directly ahead of me, loaded with bowls of peanuts and with the barstools half full. A few small tables are scattered throughout the space, and there are four TVs hanging on the walls.

The entire place feels a bit dirty, and I shiver as I pull my purse closer to me and head up to the bar. I know what Kathleen looks like from finding her on the Angry Donkey's website, and I hope that she's supposed to be working a shift today. Still, I'm a little surprised at my luck when I see her behind the bar, wiping it down with a wet rag and flicking the crumbs to the floor.

She looks terrible. I know that's a horrible thing to say about someone, but her hair is thin and limp, her eyes are sunken into her face, and she looks pale even under the blush that she rubbed on her cheeks. If I didn't know already that she's sick and needs a kidney to survive, I'd definitely wonder what was wrong with her.

Grabbing a stool, I slip onto it and try to watch her without being obvious. At first, I don't think that she sees me sitting here, but then she flips her rag over her shoulder and walks over to me, moving slowly, like every step hurts.

I swear, just watching her makes my heart break. Scott has made it so that I don't want for a single thing in my life. There's nothing in the world that I've ever wanted and had to wait to get, besides kids.

This woman has a child, but she might not make it to see her baby grow up. That thought chokes me up, and I rest my elbows on the bar, watching her.

"Hey, what can I get for you?" She leans casually on the bar and smiles at me, but I can see the lines around her eyes. She's exhausted, and I wonder how many hours she's going to have to be on her feet today.

"Just club soda and lime," I say. "If that's okay." I don't know why I suddenly feel silly ordering a virgin drink in the bar, but the kind smile she gives me instantly puts me at ease.

"Honey, you can have whatever you want in here. Doesn't matter to me whether you drink alcohol or not. Truth be told," she says, leaning forward and dropping her voice to a whisper, "I think a little water is better for you in the end. I'll squeeze some extra lime in there for you."

I instantly relax with her words and then sit back on my stool to watch her pour my drink. Some of the other people at the bar are a little rowdier than I am, but she ignores them, bringing it back to me and putting it on a napkin with a flourish.

"Thank you," I say, pulling my wallet from my purse. "How much is that going to be?"

"Don't worry about it. You look thirsty, and I'm happy to give you something to drink." She throws me an easy grin and turns to walk away, but I don't want her to go. I'm suddenly overcome with the desire to know more about her and to get to know her better.

If I'm going to give this woman my kidney, then I want to make sure that she's a good person. I'm willing to give her a kidney, but I want to know more about her first. She seems lovely, and maybe it's silly, but I have to know for sure.

"How long have you worked here?" The words spill out of me, and I'm immediately embarrassed that I asked such a personal question, but when Kathleen turns to look at me, she doesn't look upset.

"At the Angry Donkey? Off and on for years. Mostly off,

due to health problems, but I pick up shifts here and there when I feel okay. My daughter and I moved back in with my mom after I got sick, and I needed something that I could do during the day but still pick my daughter up after work. You caught me on my last shift, though. My medical problems are getting to be too much. Are you looking for a job?" Her smile reaches her eyes.

I laugh. "No, just curious. I've never been in here before. Are you okay? You mentioned health problems. I don't want to be nosy, but I can't imagine moving back in with my mom right now." I can feel the flush extending up my neck to my cheeks. I have no idea what's gotten into me. It's not like me to be so nosy with someone I just met, but I feel like I really need to get to know this woman.

"Oh, do you have all day?" Kathleen slides me a bowl of peanuts before popping one in her mouth. "Kidney problems. I knew it would eventually come to this, but I need a transplant." She shrugs like she just told me that she needs to go shopping for new socks.

If only it were that easy.

"That sounds terrible," I say, mindlessly shoving peanuts into my mouth. Maybe I can keep myself from saying something insensitive by munching on the snacks she gave me. If nothing else, it will give her time to talk, and I'll hopefully get to learn a little bit more about her.

To my surprise, Kathleen shrugs. "A lot of people have it better than me, but a lot of people have it worse. I just want to be around for my daughter as she grows up."

I think that she's about to say something else, but just then, a large man comes out the back door behind the bar. He glances around, and then his eyes fall on Kathleen.

"There you are. I got someone to come in and cover the rest of your shift for you if you wanted to head on out." He crosses his beefy arms on his chest and eyeballs her. "What is it you said you were doing?"

"Doing a little volunteer work at the school," she tells him. "You know how it goes, you offer to chaperone one afternoon party and you're the one they call every single time after that."

"A school party? Sounds miserable, so better you than me." He laughs, shaking his head. "Please tell me that as soon as you're done with that, you're going to go home and rest."

She nods firmly. Even though I'm just looking at her profile, I can see the way her jaw tightens a little bit, and I'm struck by how serious she is about this. "Of course I will, trust me. You ever been at a school party with unlimited pizza and half a dozen two-liters of soda? I'm going to be wiped out, but it'll be worth it."

"Okay, then, get on out of here. Marco will be here in a bit to finish out your shift, and I'll cover until he gets here." He sounds gruff and looks a little scary, but it's obvious that he has a soft spot for Kathleen. "It's been good working with you, Kathleen."

"You're the best, Fred." Kathleen grins at him while she unties her apron and tosses it to him. When she's sure that he's caught it, she turns to me. "Enjoy that club soda, okay? And I hope you have a really great day."

"You too," I whisper, but I'm not sure if she hears me. She's already bending to grab her purse, and then she slings it over one shoulder, turning to give me a little wave before she disappears through the same door the man came through. For a moment, all I can do is stare after her.

I didn't know what I would find when I came in here to meet Kathleen. I wasn't sure if I would feel nervous about the possibility of donating my kidney to her or more at peace, but the calm that I feel right now is almost overwhelming. Taking a deep breath, I run my fingers through the condensation on my glass before taking a sip.

If I had any doubt before about what I have to do, I don't anymore. Kathleen needs a kidney, and I'm going to give her one.

It's just the right thing to do.

6

ERIN

I feel nervous as I dial the number from the piece of paper that Scott gave me last night. After I'd gotten home from the bar yesterday, I'd texted him that I wanted to talk to this woman and at least consider giving her my kidney. He hadn't acted surprised and told me that he'd bring me her phone number when he got home from work.

Of course, by the time he got home, it was too late to call. I eyeball the clock, wondering if I'm calling too early, but then I decide that there's only one way to find out. Kathleen has a daughter, so she'll have gotten up to take her to school already.

After a complete stranger saved my life from the car accident, I've been looking for a way to really give back and help others. Seeing the billboard while on a drive with Scott and then his telling me about Kathleen are signs that it is finally time for me to do that.

When I met Kathleen yesterday, I became even more convinced that this is the right thing to do. She needs my help, and the fact that she's such an involved mom only solidifies that in my mind. The world needs more people like her.

It would be shameful for me to sit back and not help her when I know I can.

I get the last digit typed in and then take a deep breath, exhaling hard to try to calm my nerves. They're jangling, which is making it difficult for me to think, so I get up and walk around the kitchen once before sitting back down and tapping the green *Call* button.

It rings once, twice, three times, and I'm about ready to steel myself to try to leave a coherent voicemail when the ringing suddenly stops, and I hear a woman's voice in my ear.

Kathleen.

"Hello?" She sounds breathless, hopeful, and I wonder if she set up this phone number just for calls from any potential donors. That seems smart, so that you could live your life without getting excited every time your phone rang. I'd watch my kidney phone like a hawk, though, making sure to never let it out of my sight.

What if you forgot to charge it one day and a call went to voicemail? What if you accidentally missed out on the organ that would save your life because the charger slipped from the wall and your phone didn't have any juice?

"Is anyone there?"

"Hi, yes, hi." The words spill out of me, and I take a deep breath, reminding myself to slow down a little bit. This shouldn't be so stressful. It isn't a race, and it's not like I'm asking her out on a date.

No, it's worse. I'm going to offer to save her life.

"My name is Erin," I continue, speaking quickly so that she won't have time to hang up on me or interrupt me, "and my husband told me that you're looking for a kidney."

Silence. Pulling the phone from my ear, I check to make sure that we didn't accidentally get disconnected. The call is still connected, the seconds counting up on my screen. "Did you hear me?"

"Yes, thank you! I'm just . . . I wasn't sure at first if this was real life or what was going on. I'm Kathleen. Thank you for calling, Erin."

I wish that Scott were here to hear how this is going. He'd love to hear how grateful she is and hear the actual tears in her voice. I bet he had no idea that this would really happen when he told me about her. He's been nothing but supportive since I told him that I want to see if I'm a good match for her, and I'm sure he'd love to know how happy she sounds.

"Of course. I think I might be a match. We have the same blood type, and I want to find out what we need to do to make this happen for you."

For you. This is about Kathleen. I'm going to save her life, and she'll get to live a long and happy one with her daughter and her mother. Out of all of the people in the world who need a kidney, she seems like she really deserves one. I'm willing to step up and do the thing that others are afraid of.

"Thank you. So much. You have no idea. I've been praying and praying for someone to call, and I was just beginning to think it wasn't going to happen. I've been on the national transplant list for so long that you just start to believe it's never going to happen."

"Well, it's all worked out in the end," I tell her, finally settling back into my chair.

Closing my eyes, I picture her in the bar yesterday. She's younger than me, with long blonde hair that has a bit of curl in it. She looked so tired, like she wasn't sure how much longer she could keep doing what she was doing. Every movement of hers was slow, and I can only imagine how much better she'd feel if she could just rest until she found a donor.

"If you're really serious about this, then I'd love to meet you in person. Over the phone is so sterile." She laughs.

"Would you be willing to meet me somewhere? Maybe tomorrow morning for breakfast?"

"I can do tomorrow," I tell her, neglecting to tell her that I have nothing to do most of the time. Scott thinks it's hard keeping this house looking as clean as possible, but I don't do most of the work. Having a cleaning crew come in twice a week ensures that I can sit around and read or watch TV without having to be the one to scrub toilets.

I also don't mention the fact that I came into her bar yesterday. The last thing I want is for Kathleen to figure out that I wanted to check up on her and make sure that she was a really good person. I'm sure she'll figure it out eventually when we finally meet, but I don't know that I want to tell her that right now. Scott said that she was a hardworking single mom, so I figured she had to be, but I needed to know for myself. I had to make my own judgment of her character, and I did.

She's amazing and, apparently, too sick to work any longer. Someone has to help her out.

"Wonderful! Erin, thank you so much. I'm serious, I can't thank you enough for agreeing to meet and talk. The last person who called decided that it was going to be too hard on her body, and she backed out. That's why I want to meet you before we even get involved with my doctor."

Someone has already called and then backed out? I frown but manage to keep my surprise out of my voice. "I totally understand! How about eight at Black Bear Coffee? Does that sound good to you? I'll wait outside for you. I'll be wearing a red jacket."

I feel like I'm setting up a date with her. Excitement shoots through my body when she agrees.

Hanging up the phone, I carefully put it down on the table and then lean back in the chair, stretching my arms over my head. It's insane to me that someone would call her and get her hopes up, only to dash them later by backing out.

I should have told her that I'm not that type of person. She may have gotten burned in the past by someone who doesn't really care, but I care. I'm not going to get to the doctor and then suddenly change my mind.

Picking my phone back up, I turn it over and consider calling Scott to let him know what's going on. I know that he'll want an update, not only because he's excited for me to change someone's life, but also because he was a bit nervous. He worries about me, and it's sweet, but he doesn't need to.

I'm a big girl, and I can handle myself. Someone saved my life—literally kept me from dying—and I want to do that for someone else.

I'm going to make up for the people who saved me. Kathleen just happens to be the lucky person who is going to benefit.

7

SCOTT

I knew something was up the moment I came home and could smell my favorite meal cooking on the stove. The scents of chicken piccata, rice pilaf, and steamed asparagus floated out the open windows and called me into the house like I was in some kind of cartoon.

This is how Erin likes to prep me when she wants to talk about something big, and the smell of the chicken along with the size of the glass of wine she handed me when I walked in the door told me right away that she'd called the donor and wants to tell me all about it.

"How was your day?" she asks, spinning away from me to the stove.

I take her in, the spotless apron, the perfect hair, and I wonder where she called to get this food for takeout. I could probably dig deep in the trash to find the Styrofoam containers it all came in, but she likes thinking that she has her own little secrets. If she pushed it, I would tell her that it's obvious that she didn't make it since she can't even make scrambled eggs without their tasting like pieces of rubber, but that would only hurt her feelings.

Just like if she knew I was aware of the cleaning crew that came twice a week.

She thinks that she's sneaky by only using money that I deposit into her personal account in the bank. It would be easy to check her bank statements, but I don't do that in case she were to catch me. No, it's not the activity out of her account that clues me in.

It's the tiny little cameras I have set up all over the house so that I can watch her that let me know exactly what goes on in the house when I'm not here. I have to be able to keep an eye on my sweet wife. If something terrible were to happen to her, then I'm not sure what I would do with myself. Having cameras in the house ensures that I can make sure she's safe and taken care of.

She fell in love with the house when we found it, but there were some structural problems that had to be addressed before we were able to move in. While the crews were here taking care of everything, it was easy enough to have someone else come in and install cameras. They're in most every room of the house, including the large walk-in pantry that she keeps stocked with convenience meals and snacks and the master bathroom, so that I can check on her if she disappears in there during the day.

"It was good," I say, coming up behind her to nuzzle her neck. "But not nearly as amazing as coming home to this home-cooked meal. How long did it take you to put all of this together?"

She laughs and bats me away before stirring the rice pilaf. I watch her with interest when she takes a pinch of it in her fingers and tries it before sprinkling on some more salt.

I'm sure that it was perfectly seasoned when she picked it up, but she does a good job making it look like she's the one cooking.

"It's nothing, really," she finally says, grabbing the pan of chicken and pouring it into a serving bowl. I step back to give her a little room as she works. "I just know that you love this meal, and I wanted to have something special going for you when you got home."

The only thing that she did for this meal was open the bottle of wine. Not difficult, but I have to admit that she does a good job choosing a bottle to go with our meals.

"I don't know how you do it all, but you make it look really good."

She laughs and puts the food on the table.

Grabbing the white wine from the fridge, I top off our glasses and sit across from her. "Tell me, Erin, what we're celebrating, because this feels like it's something big."

Her cheeks are flushed with excitement and wine, and she leans forward, watching me as I plate my dinner. "I talked to Kathleen today, and we're going to meet up tomorrow morning for coffee."

"Wow," I say, keeping my voice as even as possible. In reality, excitement shoots through my body, but I can't let Erin know just how thrilled I am. The sooner that she moves forward with the surgery, the sooner she'll have a healthy kidney to replace the one that might fail.

And then I'll have a perfectly healthy wife. Ever since I met her, I've been working hard to make sure that she's kept as safe as possible. I'm not about to let something like a worn-out kidney stand in my way.

"Yes," she says, her voice betraying the little bit of nerves that she feels. "And before you ask, I haven't talked to my doctor yet, but I'm going to call him after I meet with her. She was just so happy that I called, Scott. I wish you could have heard it! Imagine waiting and waiting and hoping that someone will come along and save your life, and then suddenly, someone is going to, and that person is me."

She stabs a bite of chicken and eats it, still watching me.

I have nothing to say to her. Of course, I already knew about the fact that she called Kathleen and that they're meeting for coffee in the morning. I don't always listen in or watch on the cameras during the day, I'm much too busy for that, but I have them set to notify me when there's a lot of activity or loud noises, like someone talking.

So when my phone buzzed that there were voices in the house, I'd excused myself from a meeting and gone into the bathroom to listen to Erin's side of the conversation. I saw how nervous she had been and then how excited she'd gotten when she got off the phone with the woman.

I saw her call out for takeout later and then carry it all into the house, making sure that she hid the containers deep in the trash so I wouldn't find them. I saw her pick up the house a little to clean it up and then have a tiny sip of wine straight from the bottle to calm her nerves before I got home.

She was really worried to tell me that she's ready to go through with the transplant, but she doesn't need to be. There's no way I'm going to stop her, not when I'm the one who put everything in motion.

In fact, I know that there won't be any issues that may stop her from going through with this surgery. Dr. Thomas handpicked Kathleen to be the perfect match for my sweet Erin. All we have to do is perform the tests to triple-check his work and make sure that Erin is healthy enough to move forward with the transplant now.

And as for Kathleen? I know I should feel bad for her that she really isn't going to walk away from this with a new kidney, but I don't. When I questioned Dr. Thomas about how we were going to get a healthy kidney from a woman looking for a transplant herself, he told me not to worry, that he had it all figured out.

He told me about Kathleen's twin, how both that woman and Kathleen are a perfect match for my wife. She thinks she's going to give her kidney to Kathleen, but the organ will actually end up in Erin, who will be none the wiser.

She'll never know that instead of donating a kidney to Kathleen, she got a new one from the woman's twin.

I'm paying Dr. Thomas more than enough money for him to do the right thing. Money speaks, but I also know him from years ago when I defended him in court. He may not be the most aboveboard person in the world, but he gets the job done, and that's all I want for my wife.

"You know that you're probably going to have to give up drinking," I say, taking a sip. That shouldn't be a problem. I see the fire in her eyes that tells me just how badly she wants to go through with this, and I have no doubt that she's willing to do whatever it takes. Additionally, it's not like she's an alcoholic. That was my own battle to fight. I like proving to myself that I have it under control with a glass of wine here and there. If Erin were drinking, I'd have to put a stop to it, but it's good that she already wants this as badly as she does. I have to make sure that she's on the same page all the time. I've put too much work into setting up this surgery to let it all fall apart right now.

"I'm willing to do whatever it takes, so this is my last glass." She holds up her glass for me to clink it. I do, the sound of the tap ringing lightly in the kitchen. "Trust me, Scott. This is important to me."

She's grinning as she falls on her food, eating like she hasn't had a really good meal in days. I watch her for a moment, then start eating myself.

Erin may think that this is a great idea and that she's going to change this woman's life or something, but I know better. The only person who's going to walk away from this with a healthy kidney and a new lease on life is my wife.

She and I met when I was still in law school. I'd been walking to get coffee at the place across from my apartment when I saw this woman trying to help a dog off the road. It had been hit by a car, and she was sobbing, pulling on the animal, trying to move it away from the oncoming traffic.

It didn't seem to matter to her that by doing so, she was putting herself in danger. The cars didn't want to slow down or move out of the way for her. Other people didn't want to stop to help her, but I couldn't take my eyes off the gorgeous woman with long brown hair who was crying over a dog.

Forgetting the coffee, I ran across the street to help her. The dog didn't make it, and I remember the way this complete stranger fell into my arms, crying, letting me hold her tight.

I took her out to dinner that night and had a ring on her finger a month later. It didn't matter to her that I was still in law school and studying late hours. Erin was always there, always making sure that I had a hot meal for dinner and clean clothes for class. She didn't care that our dates mostly consisted of a night in while I studied.

I was just thrilled to be with her, and her with me, and now I work hard to keep her safe.

That's why I have the cameras up inside the house. It explains the tracking app on her phone and why I keep an eye on her. That's why I make sure that she goes to the doctor for a full workup three times a year. Insurance won't pay for that many visits, but I'm more than happy to cover it in cash. I just have to know that she's healthy.

EVERYONE WANTS to save the people they love. It's human nature to protect those closest to us, but not everyone in the world is willing to do what it takes.

I am.

8

KATHLEEN

bright flash of red catches my eye when I walk up
to the coffee shop, and I actually feel my body
relax.

She's here.

All night long, I was awake, wondering if she was actually
going to show up. It's easy for people to say that they want to
help, but when it really comes time to do what needs to be
done, most people are too afraid to do it. Sure, they'll open up
their wallets and give you money toward whatever experimental treatment your doctor wants to do next, but that's a
long way from donating a kidney.

Actually cutting out an organ and handing it over is on
another level. No, Erin won't be cutting it out herself, but
she's going to give me a piece of her so that I can live, and all I
can do is hope that she isn't going to get cold feet and back
out at the last second.

I need her to not back out, not only for me, but for my
daughter. Cora needs an organ just as badly as I do, and I'm
determined to do whatever I have to in order to save us both,
no matter whom it hurts.

"Hi," I say, my voice breathless, as I walk up to her. In a sea of black and gray, her red jacket stands out like a beacon, and I'm drawn to it, my feet eating up the sidewalk between us as I lift my hand in greeting.

At first, I don't think she sees me. She's looking past me, her eyes scanning the crowd as if she's looking for an old friend, and I stop, my heart beating hard in my chest, right in front of her.

Wait. I know this woman. She came in to see me at the bar the day before yesterday. Surprise washes over me, and I wonder if it was just a coincidence that she happened to show up right where I work.

Was she checking me out?

"Erin?" I ask, and her eyes snap right to my face. I suck in a breath. She's so pretty and put-together, looking more like she walked out of a magazine than like she's going to go into this coffee shop with me to get something to drink. At the bar, she was dressed like she was heading to a yoga class, but today, she looks dressed up. Even though I'm sure that this is her, for just a moment, I'm sure that I made a mistake and she's going to laugh at me, but then the spell is broken, and she smiles.

I swear, it's like the sun shines right on my face. Everything about this woman is perfect, and I instantly feel better that I dressed up for our meeting, although I do feel bad that her clothes look a lot nicer than mine do. Even with a full-time team of stylists working on me, I don't think that I could look as nice as she does.

It's not just the money for the clothes, although I'm sure that helps. She just looks . . . healthy. It radiates out of her, and I feel myself getting excited.

She's the perfect person to save me and my daughter.

"Kathleen," she says, really drawling out my name like she's from deep in the South and I'm an old neighbor or friend she hasn't seen in years. "I was looking for you, and you snuck right up on me." She pauses, and then her face lights up. "I met you the other day! Oh, my goodness, what are the odds?"

What are the odds, indeed? I stare at her for a moment longer, trying to tell whether she's being serious or not. I can't tell.

"Not a problem," I say, giving her what I hope is my best possible smile and pushing my discomfort aside. "I'm here now, and we can go talk." Stepping to the side, I grab the door to the coffee shop and swing it wide for her to go through first. She does, leaving behind a trail of perfume that's strong enough that I could follow her with my eyes shut.

Inside is packed, with the tables loaded down with not only coffee and muffins but also laptops and notebooks. More and more people are learning that they don't have to go into the office for their jobs, and they're taking advantage of that by working from home.

Or from the coffee shop, apparently.

"Oh, it's busy," I say, but Erin is already leading the way up to the counter to order. She's like Moses, parting the businessmen in suits who are clutching coffee and the teenagers who are most definitely skipping school right now.

Erin either doesn't hear me or she ignores me. Either way, in just a moment, I'm beside her at the counter, watching as she orders like she's done so a thousand times. It doesn't seem to matter how many times I go somewhere and order food. I always feel a little self-conscious doing it.

Erin doesn't. She orders us each a vanilla spiced latte and a blueberry muffin without asking me what I want. I have half a mind to say something, or at least mention what I'd prefer, but before I can work up the nerve, she turns to me, a bag with the muffins in one hand, the lattes in a carrying case in the other, and juts her chin at the door.

The command is unspoken but obvious, and I turn, weaving my way back through the coffee shop until we're outside on the sidewalk. It's immediately easier to breathe out here, and I follow Erin to a small table with two high chairs placed right under a small dogwood on the corner.

"Now," Erin says, unwrapping the muffins and handing me mine like we talked about me wanting one, "I want to get to know you, Kathleen. More than I did the other day at the bar. It's wild that you're the same person, isn't it? Tell me everything there is to know about you."

"Okay." Eyeballing her, I take a bite of my muffin and wash it down with what is probably the best latte I've ever had. Making a mental note to order one of these as a treat for myself sometime, I prepare myself to launch into the long kidney saga.

I've said it so many times to people that I think I know it by heart, but Erin lifts a perfectly manicured finger and cuts me off before I can say a word.

"I know that you already opened up to me a little bit, but I'm sure there's more to you than that. You mentioned your mom and your daughter. How are they doing? How long have you been on the list? Have you had to deal with a lot of people who offered to help you and then backed out?"

"Whoa, you have a lot of questions," I say, smiling at her. "My mom and daughter are worried, as you can imagine. And I've been on the transplant list for years, but it takes forever to find a match. And yeah, I told you that you're not the first person to call me and tell me that you can help me. It's been at least five or six." I shake my head, laying it on thick. "You have no idea what it's like to think that there's a light at the end of the tunnel for you, only to have it ripped away."

She nods, a slow movement, then takes a sip of her latte. "It sounds horrible. I can't imagine what it's like to hope that someone will help you out just out of the goodness of their heart. The other option is just hoping that someone will die and you'll be a match, and that sounds . . ."

Her voice trails off, and I'm pretty sure that I see tears glistening in her eyes. This woman is perfect. I have no idea where Dr. Thomas found her, but she's healthy, and we're a match so far. The fact that she's so willing to donate to me means that we should be able to move quickly.

It's a shame that she won't survive the donation, but I need a kidney, and so does my daughter. As wonderful as the woman across from me seems, I'm not going to put her health and well-being above my family's.

To my surprise, she reaches out across the table and takes my hand, rubbing her thumb gently across my knuckles. My first instinct is to pull back from her, but I suddenly feel like I can't move.

"No cousins who might be a match? Or siblings? Nobody who is willing to come crawling out of the woodwork to help you?" She pauses like she's a little uncomfortable, then asks, "What is wrong with your kidney, if you don't mind my asking?"

I shake my head. "Oh, you can ask. It's Alport syndrome. And as for a match . . . it's just me. There's no way that I'd ask my daughter to donate to me, not until she's old enough to make that decision, anyway, and my mom and I aren't a match. Since I don't have siblings or other close relatives, that leaves me looking elsewhere for help."

"You don't seem like the type of person to air your dirty laundry. Asking around for help from people you don't know seems . . . a little out of place for you."

I want to tell her that she doesn't really know who I am, but she obviously knows more about me than I would have thought. My cheeks flame, and I shake my head.

"I didn't want to do it," I tell her, "but my doctor made it clear to me that I don't have forever. I need to find a kidney, and sooner rather than later. He told me that he'd put out some feelers and see if we found anyone in the community who might be willing to help before I did something like set up a website or a billboard. It's embarrassing."

"It's no such thing." Her voice is firm and commanding, and I look up at her in surprise, which is probably what she wanted. "You're taking your life into your own hands, and that's something to be commended. Who knows if you would have been able to find a kidney if you hadn't gone out on a limb like this? I know that I certainly wouldn't have known that you needed help if you hadn't done that. I'm glad you listened to your doctor."

Tears sting the corners of my eyes. I never thought that there were such good people still in the world. It almost makes me feel bad about what I'm going to do to her.

Almost.

"You're going to be fine," Erin promises me, squeezing my fingers hard before letting go of my hand. "Now, let's talk about the timeline and what I'm going to have to do." Leaning back in the chair, she pats her side, right above a kidney. "This bad boy is yours. We just have to get him cut out."

That won't be a problem.

9

ERIN

I honestly feel like I'm walking on air right now. My coffee date with Kathleen went perfectly, and I asked her to send me all the information she had that I would need to make this a reality. I'm going to need doctor information, recovery information, and how quickly she thinks we'll be able to do this.

I'm sure that she wants it done as quickly as possible so that she can have a normal, healthy life, and so do I. Once I recover and I'm sure that I'm as healthy as possible again, then I think that Scott and I are going to start trying to have a family.

Besides, there's no reason to drag my feet on this. She has to want to move forward as quickly as possible. That's what I'd want, and I can't get over the fact that I'm going to be the person who can give it to her. Out of everyone in the world, Kathleen is going to trust me to save her.

She's going to have a little piece of me in her, constantly working to make sure that she's as healthy as possible. It's mind-blowing, or would be if it weren't so cool.

Turning in the kitchen, I let my eyes skim over the counters to make sure that everything is picked up before Scott gets home. I know that he's going to want to sit down tonight and talk about my meeting with Kathleen. He's so supportive, and I really couldn't ask for a better husband. Really, how many husbands would be okay with their wife donating a kidney to a complete stranger?

I'm so lucky that I have Scott. He's always told me that he's willing to do anything for me, and this just proves that. Instead of telling me to take it slow or implying that I'm making a mistake, he's right there behind me, supporting me in everything I do.

I've never been needed like this. It's strange to admit that to myself, but it's true, and I know that I'm doing something that not everyone can or would be willing to do. I'm not a mom, but anyone can get pregnant and give birth to another person. Someday, I hope I'll know what that's like, but this is totally different. It's another thing entirely to be willing to go through a major surgery so that you can give someone life.

A shiver runs up my spine as I think about what this will mean not only for Kathleen, but for me. Sure, she'll have a second chance at life, but I'll have had the chance to change someone's life. I want to help people as much as possible, and I'm finally getting the opportunity.

Kathleen told me she has Alport syndrome, but I didn't push her for more information about it, and I realize that's an oversight on my part. I was too excited to just talk to her and get to know her, but I'm sure Scott will want to know all the nitty-gritty details of what I'm doing.

It would be so easy to make something up, but I don't know the first thing about donating your kidney to someone else. All I know is that when Scott told me he'd heard about this poor woman who was looking for a kidney, I knew that I had to do something. I had to be the person to step up and help her.

Never mind that other people had promised her that they would help and then backed out. I'm not that type of person, and Kathleen doesn't need to worry about that. She doesn't need to stretch out in bed at midnight, wide awake, wondering if what she's doing is the best option or if I'm going to leave her hanging.

I don't leave people hanging. That's one thing that everyone knows about me—I'm reliable and trustworthy, and once I say I'm going to help you, I do it.

The sound of the car in the garage makes me hurry over to the stove. I didn't want to order something in for dinner tonight and try to pass it off as my own. Instead, I wanted to actually make something for Scott and me to eat. Brinner isn't anything fancy, but he never seems to care as long as I have bacon cooking.

Slitting the package and throwing some of the meat into the pan, I turn it on and then grab the eggs and cheese from the fridge to make cheesy eggs. I'm about to crack my first one into a bowl when the door from the garage swings open, and Scott strides through, his briefcase held tightly in one hand, his eyes locked on me like he already knew that I was going to be standing right here.

It's almost uncanny how he seems to know so much about me, but I think it's just because we're so connected. When you love a person the way he and I love each other, there aren't any secrets between you.

"Scott!" Putting the eggs down, I hurry over to greet him.

He kisses me, then pulls back, his eyes flicking around the kitchen like he's looking for something.

"How was your day?"

"Long," he says, putting his briefcase down and loosening his tie.

I don't know how he makes the knots on his tie always look so firm and tight. Some people's ties look like dead animals hanging around their necks, but Scott looks like he could be a model, no matter how rough his day was in the courtroom.

"I'll get you a drink." Wine with brinner might not be traditional, but he doesn't stop me from pouring him a big glass of white. When I hand it over, he sits down at the counter, eyeballing what I'm doing. "Brinner," I say in explanation, taking a sip of my water. It's cool and refreshing and just the thing I need to be drinking so I'll be as healthy as possible when it comes time to give Kathleen my kidney. "The bacon just went on, and that's why you can't smell it quite yet."

"Sounds fine. How did your coffee date with Kathleen go?" While he speaks, he coils his tie up like a snake and puts it on the counter.

I always feel like I'm on the stand with him when he asks me questions about my day, but I push that thought away. It's only because he's so intent when he listens to me. This is my husband, and he just wants to know how my day went.

Nothing more.

"It was wonderful," I tell him, cracking eggs into a bowl and grabbing the salt and pepper while I work. He likes his eggs heavily seasoned, so I shake enough pepper into the bowl to make the top of the eggs turn black before grabbing a whisk to beat them. "She needs my help, Scott. It's the right thing to do."

"You're right."

I glance up at him to make sure he's not joking. He's not. I can tell from the serious look on his face and the way his eyes soften when he looks at me. "You really think so?"

"Of course I do. Erin, you're incredible, you know that? I've never met a kinder and more caring person than you. I'm not surprised that you want to donate your kidney to Kathleen. Who else would do this for a person they didn't know?

The fact that you're so giving and selfless . . . well, it's just one of the many things that I love about you."

It feels like everything in the kitchen comes to a standstill as I look at my husband. How I got so lucky in marrying him, I'll never know. He always does what's best for our little family, so I'm sure if he's saying all of this, then he must really mean it.

"Tell me what I can do to support you." He takes another sip of his wine as he waits for me to respond, and I swallow hard, trying to think.

"I don't know, Scott." The bacon is going to burn, but I honestly can't take my eyes off my husband right now. "You're doing it. You're being supportive and asking questions and just . . . being there for me. What else could I need?"

"I won't be able to take time off work to drive you to appointments, but of course, I'll be there when you do the transplant." He squeezes my hand, and I link my fingers through his. "There's no way I'm going to let you face that alone."

"I don't deserve you," I say, but he just laughs and stands, pulling me into his arms. When I lean my head against his chest, I feel his heart hammering away, the sound comforting. "Seriously, Scott. You're too good to me."

"I knew you'd want to do this," he tells me, tracing his fingers along my jaw.

"What?" Tilting my head up, I look at him to try to figure out what he just said.

In response, he kisses me. The bacon is still sizzling away on the stove behind us, and I'm sure that it's going to burn if I don't turn it off, but I honestly don't care.

All I can do is kiss him back. He said that he'd knew I'd want to help Kathleen, which doesn't make sense, but I'll figure out what he meant by that later.

10

SCOTT

I almost slipped up with Erin last night, but she didn't catch it. I love my wife, but it's always been easy for me to distract her when I don't want to talk about something. All I had to do last night was keep kissing her and then tell her how amazing I think she is, and she never picked up on what I said.

It's obvious that she thinks she's doing the right thing, and I honestly can't believe how easy it was to convince her that donating her kidney was a good idea.

No way did I think that she would jump on the idea so quickly and be all-in after meeting Kathleen for coffee just one time. I was fully prepared to do whatever it took to convince her that Kathleen really needed her, when in reality, it seems like that was never an issue to begin with. I'm doing this for my wife, just like I do everything else for her. It doesn't matter what she needs, whether it's replacing the whole house's heating unit with one that comes with improved filters to ensure that her allergies don't bother her during the spring or finding her a kidney.

Still, I can't quite believe just how perfectly this is all

working out for me. I kept checking in on her during the day when I was gone yesterday, sneaking away from my office and pulling out my phone during court recess in the afternoon so that I could make sure she's not going to change her mind about the donation. But now, with her right across the breakfast table from me, I don't have to sneak peeks at her to try to figure out what she's up to.

My app never notified me yesterday that she was talking to someone, never picked up on loud sounds like that. Erin tends to talk to herself when she's trying to work through a problem, so the fact that my app didn't notify me meant that she wasn't doing that. She must feel at peace about giving Kathleen her kidney, which is exactly what I want.

She's obviously convinced herself that this is the right plan, which is perfect because it means that my job is going to be that much easier.

Right now, she's holding onto my wrist to keep me from leaving the kitchen table like she thinks that she's strong enough to stop me from standing up and pulling away from her. I could easily, but I don't. She's not the only one who spends their free time at the gym. I'm also putting in long hours lifting weights and running so that I look the best in my suit when I'm in front of the courtroom.

Jurors wouldn't ever admit that something like that matters to them, but it does. They're judging us by what we look like as much as by what we say and how we handle the courtroom. I'm not going to be stood up by some idiot in a cheap suit who works out more than I do, that's for sure.

But it's not an idiot lawyer I need to worry about right now. Erin isn't stupid, and I need to keep her thinking that this was all her idea.

Thankfully, after last night, she has to know that I'm fully on board with whatever she wants to do. It doesn't matter to me that the bacon burned or that we ended up ordering in pizza from the place down the street right before they closed at ten. It felt like we were dating again, eating in bed and laughing.

For the longest time, I've been carrying the burden of knowing that Erin is sick. I could tell her, sure, but I know what kind of person she is. There isn't any way that she would want to take a kidney from someone if she thought it meant that they wouldn't be able to live.

But you know what? I don't even feel bad about it. I'll do anything to keep Erin healthy, and I don't care that Kathleen's twin isn't really going to donate her kidney to her sister.

Erin needs it, and I need her healthy and whole.

Like I said, I'll do anything for my wife.

Anything.

"What are your plans for the day?" I ask Erin, taking her by the hand and bringing her fingers up so that I can give them a kiss. She looks sleepy but is dressed in workout clothes, so I assume that she's going to hit the gym after I head to work. She smiles at me, and while I wait for her to answer, I walk to the counter, pour us each a cup of coffee, stir vanilla creamer into hers, then slide hers across the table.

She takes it gratefully and blows across the surface before taking a sip. "I'm going to call the doctor and get things moving. Kathleen is desperate, and I don't want to leave her hanging. Do you think that I should call Dr. Carmen about this?"

"Your primary doctor? No, I want you to see Dr. Thomas."

She frowns. "Really? I like Dr. Carmen a lot better. Don't you think that she can help me through this instead?"

"Erin." I reach out and take her hand so that she's forced to look at me. "I know that you love Dr. Carmen, but I started having you go to Dr. Thomas last year because he's really good. He has a great reputation around town for taking care of his patients. Not only is he willing to order whatever tests you might need, but he's a transplant doctor."

"I didn't know that." She squeezes my fingers and then lets go so she can take another sip of her coffee. "Kinda weird that he'd be willing to see me this whole time, then, isn't it? It's not like I knew I was going down this path until just recently."

"He's just that good, trust me. Even if you weren't going down this path, I'd want you to go see him. I like Dr. Carmen, but she's just so . . ."

"Gossipy?" Erin laughs. "Yeah, she does like to talk during our appointments. I guess Dr. Thomas does come across as more professional."

He should, given what I'm paying him.

"There are doctor appointments, Erin. Lots of them, and I want you working with him, okay? You know that I fully support your doing this, but meet me halfway and see him instead of Dr. Carmen. Can you do that for me?"

"Oh, and you're a kidney doctor now?" There's a flirty tone to her voice. "And here I thought that I married a lawyer. Yes, Scott, if it means that much to you, I'll see him instead. He must be good for you to be in his corner like this." She stands up and gestures to the stove. "Breakfast?" When I nod, she spins away from me and grabs eggs from the fridge before cracking them into a waiting pan on the stove. The stove clicks twice before the flames turn on; then she starts stirring the eggs with a spatula, keeping her back to me the entire time.

"Thank you," I say to her, and she turns to look at me over her shoulder. "Seriously, Erin, I don't know what I'd do if something happened to you. I support you giving your kidney to Kathleen, but I have to know that you're going to be safe. I need you here in one piece when it's all said and done."

"Oh, Scott, you are the best." Leaving the stove, she comes

to me and kisses me. "I don't know what I'd do without you. Who else would be so supportive?"

And who else would buy her a kidney? *Nobody*. Nobody's willing to do what I am to keep Erin safe. I have to do everything possible to make sure that this works.

Everything I do is for her.

A few hours later, I'm in my office, flipping through files, when I get the urge to check on Erin. It only takes a few taps on my screen to pull up the house cameras so I can watch her.

What I see makes my blood run cold.

11

ERIN

It isn't until I'm on my third cup of coffee that I finally settle down on the sofa, kick off my shoes, and curl up under a blanket. I'm chilled today. It's not like it's cold in the house or like I couldn't turn on the heat if I wanted to, but I have a very good feeling that even if I were blasting the heat in here, I'd still be cold.

I think I know why, but I don't want to admit it. What Scott said last night before dinner was strange. *He knew that I'd want to do this.*

I can't wrap my mind around that, can't seem to make sense of what he said. I know I should have asked him about it this morning, but I really didn't want to bring it up. We had a lovely morning together, and after our night in bed last night, I didn't want to rock the boat.

But it's strange, isn't it? For him to say something like that to me?

I don't know. Maybe I'm overanalyzing things. Opening Instagram on my phone, I scroll mindlessly for a little while before getting bored and tapping out of it. My phone keeps popping up a warning that my storage space is running out, and if I want to install any new apps, I need to delete some things.

It's a bummer because I really want to download this new yoga app that my instructor suggested I try out. I'm pretty religious about working out, but on days like today when I can't seem to get it in gear, an app like that might be just what I need to exercise a little in the comfort of my own living room.

That means I'm going to have to delete some things, but I need to be picky about what goes. There's no way I'm going to delete the pictures that I have stored on here, nor do I want to get rid of my favorite apps. I have some for working out, for stargazing, and even one for tracking my cycle for when we decide to try to get pregnant.

There has to be some app on here that I don't use, or at least one that's pretty big and taking up a lot of space. It takes me a moment to find where I can check which apps are using the most memory, but I do and then start scrolling through the list.

I should have guessed that my music app would use a lot, but there's no way I'm going to delete that. Same goes for all of my picture storage, but then my finger hovers over an app that I don't remember installing.

TRKR

"Tracker?" I ask, tapping on the app. Immediately, a box pops up asking me for my password. "I don't remember installing this," I say, but I type in the password that I use for everything.

A red X appears on the screen, and then the app shuts back down. "That's frustrating," I say, frowning. I'm already irritated that I didn't talk to Scott this morning about the strange thing he said last night, but our morning was really nice.

He's so supportive and loving, and why would I want to

put a damper on that? At the same time, I'm annoyed with myself because I can't help the tiny whispers of doubt about what I'm doing in the back of my head.

I know that Kathleen needs me and that I can help her, but I'm scared. What if I'm rushing into this? What if I should take some time to get to know Kathleen better?

I don't have time to think about that right now, though, not when dealing with this damn app. I tap on it to open it again and try my password without the string of numbers on the end of it that Scott promised me would make it safer.

Another big red X.

"Okay, now you're pissing me off." I'm getting hot now, and I flip the blanket off me and onto the floor before adjusting my position on the sofa. Three more times, I try to open the app to see what it is, but I can't. "I'll just delete you, then," I say, holding my finger down on the screen until the option to delete pops up.

With a sigh, I tap it, but another red X appears on the screen.

"What the hell?" Groaning, I rub my hand over my eyes when my phone rings. I wasn't expecting a call, and I jump when it vibrates in my hand. It's just Scott, and I give my head a little shake before answering it. "Hey, honey. What's going on?"

"I could ask you the same thing." He sounds flustered and takes a deep breath. "I just wanted to see how you're doing."

I frown, readjusting on the sofa. "It's actually weird that you called right now. I was trying to clear some memory on my phone, but I can't get this one app to delete. I keep trying, but it says that my password is wrong."

"That is weird. You sure it's not hardware on the phone? You can't delete something like that because the entire phone will crash and stop working."

"I didn't know that." I want to look at the screen, but I have the phone pressed up to my ear. "I feel kinda silly now."

"No, don't. If you don't know, then you don't know. I've run into that before with electronics. They pack phones and computers so full of operating system stuff and other junk that it can slow things down. It's called bloatware, if you want to look it up, but there's nothing to learn because there's really nothing that you can do about it."

"Oh. That's really frustrating. Do I need a new phone, then?"

"Yeah, I think you should go ahead and order one. You know that I've been telling you for a while that it's time to get a new phone that will be faster for you. Hell, you can order it today if you want, and as soon as it comes in, I'll help you transfer everything over."

I let out a sigh of relief because Scott knows that doing that is my least favorite part of having a new phone. Sure, there's nothing like the fresh new screen free from scratches, and the fact that you can download whatever you want without worrying about running out of storage space, but you still have to transfer everything, and that's a royal pain in the butt.

"After the transplant," I say. "That'll be a nice treat."

"Whenever you want. I know that it's tempting to keep messing with it, but you're not going to do anything good, okay? Even if you do manage to delete the app, all it's going to do is destroy your operating system."

"Damn. Okay. It's just weird. The name, that is."

He pauses. "What's it called?"

"TRKR." I spell it for him.

"Oh, I've heard of that." He's back to sounding confident, like I'm sure he does when he's in the boardroom. "You know how you can see on a map when getting directions where the bad traffic is? That's what that's for."

Scott always knows how to make things make sense for me. I'm sure there are some women with spouses who make fun of them for not knowing stuff like this, but Scott is always kind about it. I'm really lucky.

"You're the best," I tell him, snuggling deeper into the sofa. I wasn't feeling great when I sat down on the sofa, but talking to him makes everything better. In fact, I don't even know why I was concerned about what he said. All he was saying was that he knew I'd want to help Kathleen because that's who I am.

That's all.

And he's right. Scott knows me and my heart so well.

"I love you, Erin, but I have to get back to work. Have a good rest of your day, okay?"

"I love you." Squeezing the phone tightly, I wish that he were here with me. "Thanks for explaining that to me."

"Not a problem." He's gone, and I'm left with a warm feeling in my chest.

How lucky am I that he called right when I had a question? Turning off my screen, I toss the phone next to me on the sofa. Lucky. That's me.

Still, there's a strange thought in the back of my mind that I can't seem to get rid of.

I'm lucky, sure, but how did Scott know that I needed his help with something?

12

SCOTT

Relief floods through me when I hang up the phone and then tap straight back to the cameras. Erin's snuggled up on the sofa where she was when I first saw her angrily tapping at her screen. It had taken me a moment to zoom in and see what it was that had her so upset, but as soon as I saw it, I knew I had to put a stop to it.

She was trying to delete my tracking app from her phone. I don't know how the hell she found it or why I'm so lucky that she's as gullible as she is, but the last thing I was going to do was sit here and watch her try to figure out what it was.

She can't delete it, of course, not without the password that I set up for the app when I installed it, but she could ask questions. She could research the app online to find out what it is. The creators did a good job of hiding their tracks, so a simple Google search wouldn't turn anything up, but if she went to the right message boards, she'd find it.

And I can only imagine the fallout.

My breathing slows down, and I try to force myself to relax. Sure, there was almost a crisis, but I stopped it. Erin won't question me, I'm sure of it. She never has, and there's no reason she should start now. I'll just have to keep checking in on her more than I have just to make sure that she doesn't try anything.

My blood runs cold when Erin suddenly looks straight up at the wall. At the same time, a popup appears on my screen.

Battery low.

Shit. First the tracking app and now she's looking right at the camera? What are the chances that I forgot to charge the camera last night and it chose right now to start blinking its low-battery light?

It's the only one that isn't hardwired directly into the house because I didn't have time to get an electrician in to do the work and then repair the holes in the wall before she would find it. It runs on battery power, and I have to pull the entire thing out of the vent once a month, replace the batteries, and then put it back up.

And I forgot.

It must have beeped as well as flashed a light, or something, because it definitely caught my wife's attention.

Erin's getting closer, her face growing in size on the screen, and I panic. I need to get home, need to get her away from the camera. Stabbing at the screen, I shut the camera off, which should stop the blinking light warning of a low battery. As soon as that's done, I pick up the phone and call my wife.

"Pick up, pick up, pick up," I mutter, pacing around in my office. I'm sweating, and I grab the collar of my shirt, yanking it out from my neck to try to get a little more air.

"Scott? Is everything okay?" Erin sounds confused, and I know I need to make a fast decision about what I'm going to do.

I can't stay here and watch as she gets closer to figuring it all out. I have to do something.

"I'm taking you out for lunch," I tell her, grabbing my suit jacket from the back of my chair and throwing it over my shoulder. "Get dressed for someplace nice."

She laughs, a nervous sound, and the hair on the back of my neck sticks straight up. "What in the world has gotten into you? You're the one who always tells me that you can't skip out on work or you're going to get eaten alive in the courtroom."

"I want to see you," I tell her, stalking toward my office door. If I can keep her on the phone, then I'll be able to hear if she's getting close to the camera. As soon as she gets off, I won't know what she's doing unless I watch her on another camera. "Put on something nice. I'm taking you out; then we're having a repeat of last night."

She pauses, and I know that she's reliving last night. That will make her do what I want, I'm sure of it.

"You mean it?" Her voice is lower, huskier.

"Every word." Throwing open my office door, I'm ready to walk out into the hall when Alexander appears, a stack of folders in his hands, a look of doom and gloom on his face. "Fuck," I mutter.

"What?" Erin asks at the same time that Alexander speaks.

"I need your help. Just ordered some delivery for lunch so we can get this done. I have that big case coming up, and they just dropped new evidence on me. I won't be able to get through it without you."

My heart sinks. Helping Alexander work through lunch is absolutely the last thing I need to be doing right now, but from the look on his face and the way he's pushing past me into my office, I'm not going to have a choice.

"Scott? Is lunch canceled?" Erin sounds sad, and I close my eyes, swearing silently to myself.

"I'm so sorry, honey," I tell her. My skin feels too tight right now, like I need to rip it off to get some air to breathe. I can't just be at the office if she's going to be looking for the camera.

What if she finds it?

"It's okay." Erin sounds defeated. "I'm sure I can find something here."

"No." I sound panicked, and I can tell that Alexander hears it in my voice by the way he raises his eyebrows. I turn away from him, wanting at least a little privacy while I talk to my wife. "No, that's not fair to you. I'm getting something ordered in, and I promised you a nice meal. Go out to lunch, Erin. You deserve it."

"No, it's fine. Seriously, Scott, you don't need to feel bad. I know your job can pop up like this, and you have to handle stuff. Don't worry."

"I am worried." I rack my brain, trying to think about how I'm going to get her out of the house. I can't have her sitting around or, worse, digging around. Sure, the living room camera is turned off, but what if she gets curious again? I'll have to move it when I get home.

"I'm a big girl," she says, laughing.

"I know, but I like to take care of my girl. How's this? You get dressed, and I'll come pick you up in half an hour and take you someplace nice, okay? It'll be like you're a rich, old, fancy lady with a driver."

She hesitates, and I'm sure that she's going to say no, but I continue.

"I love you, Erin. Let me do this to take care of you."

"Okay," she says, and relief floods through my body. It's short-lived, though. I have to get home as quickly as possible and get the camera out of the vent before she sees it. I can do it.

I have to.

13

KATHLEEN

It takes until noon the day after my coffee shop meeting with Erin for my doctor to finally call me back. It's ridiculous, if you ask me. I know that Dr. Thomas is a busy man and has lots of things to do, but I'm the one who needs the kidney to live. Why he's dragging his feet and not getting back to me faster is beyond me.

It's not like he's doing all the legwork. Sure, he had to find Erin and make sure that she would be a good match, but it can't be that hard. I'm the one who had to go out to the coffee shop with her to really seal the deal. I'm the one who had to sit there and act like multiple people had already backed out on helping me.

It was obvious that Erin has more money than sense, but I still had to be the one to sit there and really stroke her ego to ensure that she felt as terrible for me as possible, like I'm someone in need of saving. But I'm not. Never in my life have I sat back and let someone else run the show.

When I found out that my kidney was failing, I knew I had to take control. And when I realized that I couldn't let my daughter, Cora, go through the same thing, I was the one who found a doctor with more greed than morals who would be willing to do the double transplant and leave Erin without a kidney.

Sure, I should feel bad for her. Dr. Thomas had seemed surprised at my idea at first, but when I told him that there would be plenty of money in it for him, he quickly changed his tune. So yes, he found Erin, and he's the one who did the tests to ensure that she'd be a good match for both me and Cora, but I'm the one who had to look her in the eye and get her to really feel bad for me.

And still, I'm a little shocked that it's actually going to work. Erin wants to go through with this, and I never thought that Dr. Thomas would find someone so willing to help me this quickly. She wants to lie there and get sliced open just so that a piece of her can go into me and save my life. Tons of people have some fantasy about doing something selfless like this, but Erin is the first person I think will really go through with it.

She just has no idea how much work it will really be. Nobody does, which is why I was so worried when she and I met for coffee yesterday. Sure, Dr. Thomas had done his best to reassure me that she was all-in and wasn't going to back out on me, but it's still hard to trust someone you barely know.

Which makes me wonder about how she just so happened to show up in the bar where I was working. It's a strange coincidence, and I don't believe in those. She seemed so out of place, so nervous, and at first, I had just chalked it up to her being in a new place for the first time, but it almost felt like more.

The thought makes me shiver, but I push it away, unwilling to give it any more of my time and energy. Erin couldn't have known who I was because that would mean that she was checking up on me, and I can't see why she would do that. She's a sweet woman, if a little naïve.

My phone buzzes, and I pick it up, excitedly pressing it up against my ear. "Dr. Thomas," I say, his name like a prayer on my lips. This is why doctors get such big heads—they know that people worship the ground they walk on. Just a simple phone call from a doctor is more than enough to make me talk lower, to move slower, like I'm in the presence of someone truly holy.

And they know it.

"Kathleen, I had a message on my desk that you have good news for me. Did you meet with the donor?"

"I did. Erin. She's perfect," I say, the words spilling out of me. I don't want to come across as too needy right now, but he has to know that he found the perfect donor for me. Erin is not only a match, but she's more than willing to do whatever needs to be done to save my life.

She just doesn't know that she's also going to get to save Cora's.

"You didn't do anything to screw this up, did you? Anything to make her doubt what she's doing? I can't have you messing this up, Kathleen."

Like I don't know what's riding on all of this.

When I close my eyes, I can see Erin sitting right across from me at the coffee shop. I see the way her face lit up when I told her how thankful I was that she was willing to help me. I remember in detail how she nodded along when I mentioned tests, and waved away my concerns about how quickly we could get started.

"I don't think she'll back out," I tell him. "And as for when we can get started, I think we can do it anytime." Somewhere deep inside me, I know it's the truth. Erin is ready. I know it.

"Good. That's great, Kathleen. Wonderful work meeting her and making sure that you really sold her on the donation. I'll get in touch with her and have her come in to my office as soon as possible. You know that we're on borrowed time right now, so if she has any concerns, any doubts, you need to squash them. Do you understand? I'll perform the transplants, but you have to make sure that she doesn't get cold feet."

"I understand," I whisper, then swallow hard. "I'll do whatever I have to so I can make sure that she shows up."

"Good." He hangs up.

I sit there for a moment, my phone still pressed up against my ear, the empty sound of silence flowing over me like a river. This is happening, and it's all up to me to keep things in motion.

Dr. Thomas's words ring in my ear. *You know that we're on borrowed time right now.*

So true. I had no idea just how precious time could really be. I had no idea that I'd be fighting against it every second of the day, doing whatever I could to slow it down.

I glance down at my watch, then press its face against my ear. The ticking is quiet, but it's still there, and I feel a wave of calm wash over me. Time moves so quickly, and I'm willing to do whatever it takes to slow it down for me and for my daughter. When I'm stressed during the day, I press my watch up against my ear and take a few deep breaths.

The constant ticking helps keep me grounded.

"What did the doctor say?" A voice from the living room pulls me out of my thoughts, and I stand, groaning a little bit when I do, then walk from the kitchen into the living room. It's dark in here with the curtains drawn, and before answering, I walk over and yank them open, allowing sunlight to stream into the room.

My energy levels have been decreasing for a while now. At

first, I chalked it up to stress and not getting enough sleep while pulling long shifts at the bar, but this is a classic symptom of my disease and one that I know isn't going to get any better until I have a transplant. A new kidney is going to be the only thing to save me now.

It'll stop the fatigue, the fifteen pills a day I have to take, the swollen calves, and even the hearing loss. Anyone who thinks that Alport syndrome isn't so bad hasn't ever had to live with it. I grew up watching my mom suffer with it and dealing with it myself. So far, Cora doesn't show any signs of being sick, but that's why I want to take care of her now, before she does.

"He said that we don't have a lot of time and that I need to get the donor in right away to start with tests." Pushing my mom's legs out of the way, I sit down on the end of the sofa. She has the TV on, but it's muted so that she can still watch her soaps without their being too loud while I'm puttering around in the house.

"And you really think that this woman will go through with it? She doesn't know you. What does she stand to gain from helping someone she doesn't know?"

I sigh. This is what I just went over with Dr. Thomas, and I don't want to have to go through it again. "Trust me, Mom, she's not going to back out. Everything is going to work out just fine."

I have to believe that it is. I've been dreaming of getting a healthy kidney since I was a teenager and first diagnosed with Alport syndrome. It's done its best to steal as much of my life from me as possible, and I'm tired of it. It's time to take back my life.

One transplant for me wasn't enough. Sure, there are many patients who get a new kidney and are healthy again, but not me. It's just my luck that my first transplant is failing.

I have to have another one, and I have to make sure that Cora never wastes away on the transplant list.

Dr. Thomas found the one person in the world I think we can con into giving me what I need. She decided that she was going to help me. She'll give me what I need to survive. A kidney.

But not just one.

14

ERIN

Nerves keep my knee bouncing up and down while I wait for the doctor to call me back to an exam room. It's a quiet office and situated a little out of town, which is probably why most people drive right on by it without paying attention. I've been here before, but I really look at it today. The squat gray building doesn't exactly make me feel inspired that the doctor working inside is the best in the area, but I guess that not all of the world's doctors can work in the huge hospital right downtown.

Besides, I trust Scott. If he's telling me that Dr. Thomas is the best doctor in the area for transplants and that he'll make sure everything goes smoothly, then I have no reason to believe he's not telling me the truth. Everything that Scott does is to keep me happy and safe, and I have to remind myself not to judge the good doctor based on the location and appearance of his office.

More than that, judging by the way that Kathleen dressed and carried herself, she doesn't have the money or the insurance to go to one of the more expensive offices in the middle of downtown. They're all built with huge glass windows that take up entire walls, lighting that seems straight out of a sci-fi book, and landscaping that would put the White House to shame. It seems like Dr. Thomas really isn't interested in spending all of his money on stuff like that, which tells me that he's more focused on taking care of his patients.

A lot of caring doctors do pro bono work. I first learned about that with Scott when he was helping clients by offering them reduced rates or even free representation. It had surprised me at first, but he told me it's a fairly common practice among lawyers and doctors to help people out when they simply can't afford the care they need.

I bet that's what this is. I bet that Kathleen is working with Dr. Thomas because he was willing to cut her a deal. She needed help, and I'm sure all of the tests and workups that she's had done so far aren't cheap. Dr. Thomas probably cuts her a deal and then writes it all off on his taxes.

And then he goes home at night to his perfect little family, and his wife tells him how kind he is to help out people who don't have nearly as much as they do. That's what this is. Scott does the same thing sometimes, taking on pro bono cases for people who tug at his heartstrings and can't afford the ridiculous fee that lawyers charge.

I'm used to how this all works, and now that I understand exactly what's going on here, I feel like I can relax some. I'm just finding a comfortable position on the hard plastic chair in the waiting room when an older woman in scrubs leans out from the door across the room and calls my name.

Standing, I'm well aware of how my heels click on the hard tile floor in the empty room as I walk to her, but I don't have time to worry about the sound I'm making. I'm here for Kathleen.

"Erin Anders?" the nurse asks, then holds the door wide for me when I nod. "Great, why don't you come down here to the end of the hall with me, and Dr. Thomas will be in as quickly as possible to talk to you about the procedure and what tests you're going to have to do."

"How long will the process take?" She's walking fast in her little white rubber shoes, and I have to hurry to keep up.

"Today? Not too long. An hour or so."

"No, I mean before we can do the transplant." Lowering my voice, I grab the nurse's arm so that she'll slow down and turn to look at me. "Kathleen is amazing, but it's obvious just from looking at her that she doesn't have a whole lot of time left. I'm sure she'll feel so much better once she has my kidney."

"Of course," she says, gently pulling her arm out of my grasp. "Why don't you take a seat in here, and Dr. Thomas will be in shortly to talk to you about everything. I'm sure he can put your mind at ease and will be able to answer all of your questions, okay?"

"Sounds great." I push past her into the small room and take a seat on a chair in the corner. I'm not going to sit on the exam bed unless he asks me to. Sitting on them always makes me feel like I'm some sort of animal on display. The nurse closes the door, and I wait for a moment before pulling my phone from my purse to check the time.

I'm running late but on my way! Tell Dr. Thomas I got caught at my daughter's school at pickup.

The text from Kathleen makes me frown. We got so busy talking yesterday that it never crossed my mind to find out more about her family. That's not like me. I usually do everything I can to learn about other people to set them at ease. My nerves must be worse than I thought they were. I wonder how old her daughter is.

Young enough to need to be picked up from school, that

much is clear, but that doesn't really narrow it down very much. I make a mental note to ask Kathleen when I see her.

I know we're not going to suddenly become best friends just because I'm giving her my kidney, but I can't help but feel like I want to take care of her a little bit. She's probably only ten years younger than I am, but she obviously needs someone on her side. There's no reason it can't be me.

No reason the two of us can't form some sort of relationship when this is all said and done. Sure, Scott has told me that he wants to have kids with me, but what if we're too late by the time we finally get started? That thought has crossed my mind before and honestly scares me.

It's not that Kathleen would ever take the place of a future child that we may have, but I still feel some connection with her. I want to take care of her, and I want to show her that there's someone on her side who is willing to go out on a limb to keep her safe.

From our one coffee date, I really like her. Sure, she was a little nervous at first when we started talking, but I can't blame her. I would have been scared to death if I were in the same situation. How many people did she say had offered to donate a kidney to her and then backed out? Too many.

Kathleen had no way of knowing if I was serious about wanting to help her or if I was just morbidly curious about what she was going through. She had to be a little nervous to open up to me, but that will all change. It may be silly, and I'm not sure what Scott will say, but I want more of a relationship with her.

I want to take her shopping, show her how to do her hair so that she looks and feels great, and even take her and her daughter to museums. Judging by how she dresses, I doubt that there are extra nickels in her pocket for trips to the zoo or to see a play.

Now I'm excited. I want to get to know her more, not just

because I'm going to donate my kidney to her but because I think that we'd really get along. I bet we'd be great friends, given the chance.

I just hope that she feels the same way. It's silly that I'm so nervous about what she'll think of me, but I don't want this relationship to end after the surgery. We're so different, but way down deep, I think that we're more alike than we may seem at first.

"I barely know her, yet I'm willing to do whatever it takes to save this woman," I whisper to myself. That feels good. She's in a terrible position, but I'm going to help her get out of it, and then the two of us are going to have a wonderful relationship, I can tell.

How many people would do that? None, apparently. I'm the first one to actually be willing to go through with this. I'm not sure what that says about me, but I'm doing the right thing. I know I am.

Everything she's doing is to make sure that her daughter can have as wonderful a life as possible with her still around, and I'm going to help make that happen.

What a good mom she is. I can only imagine how hard it was to talk to me at the coffee shop without telling me how scared she was that she might leave her daughter behind. She doesn't have to tell me how scary it is because I'm going to make sure that she never has to face that fear.

My mind is made up. I know Scott is more supportive than I could ever imagine, and I'm sure that what I just figured out will put any concerns that he may have at ease. Kathleen needs me, but more than that, so does her daughter.

I'm not going to let either of them down. I don't care what the doctor needs me to do. I'll do anything.

15

SCOTT

It's been four days since Erin met with Kathleen, and we're just now sitting down to talk about things again. It's been a busy few days at work, which is why I offered to take her out to dinner tonight so we could connect and relax while someone else cooked the food and took care of the dishes for us.

She won't be scurrying around the kitchen, making sure that we're both happy, and that means we should have plenty of time to talk. I managed to get us a reservation at Flight, one of the nicest restaurants in town. There are very few places around here that have a dress code diners have to abide by, and this is one of them. That's why I kept my suit from work on and refreshed my tie and why Erin dressed up in a slinky dress that I haven't seen her wear in years.

She looks stunning, as usual. That's one thing I appreciate about Erin. Unlike some of the other lawyers' wives, who have access to a lot of money from their husbands but don't know how to spend it to look their best, Erin always looks put together. It's expensive to keep her looking so nice, but I don't mind.

I see the way other men in the restaurant turn to look at her as we walk by. I notice the way the waiter hiccups a little bit when he sees her sitting there across from me. Is it vain?

Sure.

Would I change it?

Not for the world.

"Tell me what's on your mind," I say to her, gesturing for the waiter to bring me some water. He's hovering nearby and hurries to our table to refresh my glass. "You haven't touched your cocktail. Do you not like it?"

"I'm sure it's great." Erin runs her finger along the rim of the glass. "But I can't drink now. I'm about to start a lot of tests, and they need my kidneys to be as healthy as possible to make sure everything goes smoothly."

"Darling, it's virgin." I smile at my wife and reach out to take her fingers. "You really don't think that I would order you alcohol knowing that you have the transplant coming up, do you?"

She beams at me. "I should have known. You're so good to me. I just want to take this as seriously as possible, and I'm willing to do whatever I have to so I can make sure this works. I told you that she said she'd had some people tell her that they'd donate a kidney only to back out later. I'm not going to be that person."

"You're not that type of person, so I don't think that you even need to worry about it. Erin, I can't imagine your ever doing something that would hurt another person. Are you feeling nervous about the tests? Do you want to talk about them?" She'd left out a list of various tests she'd have to go through on the counter last night, and I saw it when I wandered downstairs to get a cup of coffee this morning before my shower. I'm not sure if she left it there on purpose for me to find or if I accidentally happened upon it, but the result is the same.

I just have to make sure that she's not going to try to back out of this. If she tries, then I'll have to stop her. I have to make sure that she goes through with this, no matter what it takes.

She flushes, and I have my answer. "There are definitely more tests than I would have thought," she agrees, obviously choosing her words carefully. "But it's all worth it. Did you know that of the six thousand or so people who get a kidney transplant in the US each year, only around eight hundred come from family members?"

"Most of the rest are donated after death, huh? Or is there some big underground movement to donate your organs to someone you don't know?"

This makes her smile, and I relax, taking another sip of water.

"I think some people are just driven to do it," she says, staring right at me. "And as for the tests, they're no worse than Kathleen will have to go through to get my kidney. Dr. Thomas took blood from me last week to make sure my kidneys and liver are healthy, and he did a thing called a crossmatch test. We're just waiting on the results from that, but I figure no news is good news."

"What's that test?" I'm honestly interested in what she has to say. Sure, I've done my research and looked up what's going to happen to her. I did all of that as soon as I found out that her kidney wasn't healthy. Still, it's been a little while, and I want to make sure that I know exactly what's going on when she's with Dr. Thomas.

"They mix together our blood to make sure that they're a good match." She wiggles her fingers in the air at me to show me what she means.

"Sounds like a wrestling match."

Another laugh. She reaches for her drink and takes a sip while she looks at me. "This is actually really good. Fruity.

And yes, something like a wrestling match. Anyway, enough about me. This will take a while, like you said, so there's plenty of time to talk about it. How's work? And when do you think our food will get here? I'm famished."

I don't have much to say about work, mostly because it's the same old thing day in and day out. As a criminal defense attorney, you'd think that I have a lot of interesting cases to handle all the time, but most of them are the same. After working for the district attorney for a few years out of law school, I decided to switch teams, as they say, to defend the same type of people I used to put behind bars.

Why? Because they pay better, that's why. Is it terrible that I'd rather defend someone who drove drunk and killed an innocent pedestrian than put them in jail? Quite possibly. In fact, this was a huge conversation that Erin and I had when I told her I wanted to make the switch.

But I'd rather live in a nice house in a nice neighborhood where I don't have to worry about someone breaking in and stealing the silver than be so poor that I live right next to the people I put in jail. Not only would I be worried all the time about someone breaking into our house, but if I did manage to put someone in jail, I didn't want to live next to their family.

More than any of that, though, working as a defense attorney means that I can afford this transplant. I can pay for whatever Erin needs to be as healthy as possible. If I were still with the district attorney, there'd be no way I could afford Dr. Thomas's fee for her transplant.

"Work is good," I tell her. "I'm going to be living at the office this week while I work on a big case, but I'm going to do my best to make it home in time for dinner. No guarantees, of course."

"The Smith murders?" Erin perks up a little bit. I know that I shouldn't talk to her about the particulars of all the cases I have, but they're just so interesting. And it's one thing that will draw her attention away from whatever show she's watching on TV, so it's always nice to have her full attention for a while.

"Yep." I nod, then lean back in my chair while the waiter sets our steaks in front of us. Mine is rare, and Erin's is medium, but besides that, we order the same thing. "So I'm sorry, but I won't be home until late some nights. Don't worry about dinner. I'll let you know if I'm going to be late and just order something in to the office, okay?"

She nods and takes a bite of her steak, moaning a little as the flavor hits her tongue. "Sounds good. I'll keep you up to date about appointments with the doctor, okay?"

"Thanks." She grins at me, and I smile back. I don't need her to worry about letting me know what's going on with the appointments. I'll know just by keeping an eye on her during the day, but it's nice that she wants to make sure that I'm included.

If Erin ever knew about the cameras in the house and the tracking app on her phone, I'm sure she'd lose her shit.

That's why she can't ever find out.

16

KATHLEEN

Cora sits in the back seat, her eyes locked straight ahead on the road, her hands clenched into fists at her sides. She's completely ignoring the pack of chips on the seat next to her and doesn't seem to care that they're about to slide off the seat and fly all over the floor if she doesn't grab them the next time I stop.

That's why I tap my brakes a little bit harder than I need to at the next red light. I'm watching in my rearview mirror as they go flying, which is why I see her glare at me before turning to stare out the window instead of picking them up.

"If you hadn't left them on the seat next to you, then they wouldn't have fallen all over the floor," I tell her, and I'm met with an icy silence. That's one thing that Cora is really good at—ignoring me or making me out to be the bad guy. All I did was tap the brakes to keep from running the red light by accident.

It's not my fault that she didn't hold onto her snack, and it's certainly not my fault that she's now going to have to pick them all up off the floor so they don't crunch into tiny little pieces.

"You slammed on the brakes on purpose," she says, which is more than she's said to me since we left the doctor's office. "I know you did."

Everyone told me that the twos were terrible, and then after that, having a kid would get a lot easier, but they neglected to mention that when they turn fourteen, girls get sassy. And rude.

"I'm sorry," I tell her, searching for her eyes in the rearview mirror. "I didn't mean to, honestly. Are we going to fight about it all the way home?"

"Home?" She looks straight at me. "I thought you were going to take me back to school. I don't want to miss the entire day. Why do I have to go home?"

"Honey, it takes a lot out of you to have your blood drawn for appointments. Trust me, I know. It's better just to go home and rest right now so your body can heal."

"It was a tiny blood draw. Three vials, Mom. Don't be ridiculous."

"Dr. Thomas thinks that you should go home and rest," I tell her, ignoring her tone even though I want to snap at her to stop talking to me like that. "So that's what we're going to do. It's best to listen to him, Cora. He knows what he's talking about."

"But I feel fine." She crosses her arms on her chest and glares at me. Luckily for me, the light turns green, and I press down on the gas, ignoring the way she's staring at me.

I don't have to look at her right now, but that doesn't mean I can't still feel her eyes boring into the back of my head. She's doing everything she can to make her point clear that she's unhappy, but I don't care. When I became a mom, I swore to myself that I would do whatever it took to protect her and keep her healthy and safe.

That's why I'm taking her home right now and not letting her go back to school to run and play.

"I know you do, darling, but you'll be glad you rested. Trust me. After these types of appointments, all I want to do is go home and sleep. Besides, Grandma will want to hear all about it."

"Great. I'll tell her that Dr. Thomas took my blood and sent it off for labs. I'll tell her that I want to be at school, not watching soap operas with the closed-captioning on and the sound turned way down. Excuse me for wanting to go and be with people my own age."

Enough. Her words echo and bounce around in my head, and I grit my teeth together as I pull the car off the side of the road. Slamming my finger onto the button to turn on the hazard lights, I whip around in my seat to look at her. Cora looks surprised that I'd pull off the road like this, but I really want to make my point clear.

"Stop it. You need to be healthy, Cora, and I'm willing to do whatever it takes to keep you feeling your best. I'm sorry that you want to go to school, but when the doctor says you need to rest, then you need to rest. Your kidney—"

"*Your* kidney! You're the one having a transplant, Mom, not me! I'm not the one with Alport syndrome!"

"Not yet! But you're going to start feeling bad, I know you are!" The words fly from my lips, and I slam them shut, closing my eyes for a brief moment so I can try to control my temper. Getting angry with Cora doesn't solve anything. She's at the age where she's going to push back against what I tell her no matter what I do, and I need to try to stay calm.

Where did my sweet little girl go? I've done everything I can to keep her loving and kind, yet she's growing out of what I feel like I can control sometimes. Nobody ever told me that being a parent would be so difficult. I knew, deep in my heart, that being a single mom would be the most challenging thing I'd ever do, but it's still hard to go through it.

Knowing something and dealing with it on a daily basis are two entirely different things.

"Cora," I say, making sure that my tone is even and tempered and she can't tell just how frustrated I am with her right now, "I know it doesn't seem fair, but the doctor said there are signs that you're getting sick, too."

"Like what? What signs? I feel fine."

I shake my head. "No, baby, you don't. I see when you're fatigued and have trouble getting up and moving. I know that PE at school is harder for you than it is for other kids."

She's silent, and I risk a glance back at her in the rearview mirror. Her arms are crossed on her chest, and she's staring at me like she's never hated me more in her life.

Fine. She can hate me all she wants, but I'm the only person who knows the signs to look for in her. I'm the only person in her life who's willing to do what it takes to keep her healthy and safe. I know she hates it when I worry, but how could I not?

She's my daughter, and I know what kind of terrible life is ahead of her if she doesn't stay healthy. I don't want her to end up on a kidney transplant list, hoping that someone will die so that she can have a little bit longer to live. I especially don't want her to have to work with some shady doctor who's willing to go out of his way to find a donor.

I saw that billboard with the woman begging for a kidney. There's no way I'll let my daughter sink to the depths of having to try to tug on the heartstrings of people while they're driving to and from work.

Working with Dr. Thomas and sucking up to Erin is frustrating, but I'm willing to do it. Not only for me, even though I am excited to go through with the surgery. I can't wait to feel better, to know that I'm not going to be so tired. Even though I can tell that Cora doesn't always feel good, she still has a lot more energy than me.

I can't wait to keep up with her. To not have to take all the medication that I currently do just to be able to make it through the day. Cora has no idea how difficult my life is right now when I don't feel good.

And if everything goes to plan, she'll never have to know.

17

ERIN

I get the call that my blood work all looks good and that my crossmatch test with Kathleen's blood was perfect when I'm up to my elbows in the raised garden bed in the backyard.

I'd begged Scott to have someone come to the house and build a raised bed for me so that I could grow some herbs for the kitchen. Even though I don't like to cook, there's nothing that makes something seem homemade faster than sprinkling some fresh herbs on top of the meal after it's been plated.

I'm pretty sure it's my fresh supply of parsley, basil, thyme, oregano, and even chives that keep Scott believing I'm the one turning out such delicious meals every day.

If he knew the truth, he'd be destroyed. When we got married, we promised to love each other and honor each other. It's not my fault that I'm a nightmare in the kitchen, that burning myself in the oven isn't my idea of a good time, and that I'd much rather read a book or go shopping than work over a hot stove all evening, every single night.

So I started ordering takeout and dressing it all up with herbs once a week to give me a break. Once a week turned into twice a week, which turned into three times, and now I'm in it so deep that if Scott ever really pays attention to where I spend the grocery money, I'm sure that he'd figure it out in a second.

Luckily for me, he's way too involved at work to pay attention to the fact that I rarely go grocery shopping. I know that a lot of wives hate it when their husbands work all the time, but I don't have a problem with it.

Of course, I miss him like crazy when he's not home, but it just means that our time together is that much better when he's around. It's not his fault that he's such a good lawyer and in such high demand.

Besides, when I do get him all to myself, he makes me feel amazing.

My phone starts to ring, and I wipe my hand on my jeans before remembering that I have gloves on and ripping one off and tossing it to the side. The number is local, but I don't recognize it, and I take a deep breath before swiping on the screen.

"Hello? This is Erin."

"Erin, this is Tracy Jones at Dr. Thomas's office. I just wanted to let you know that since the crosshatch test came back just fine, you're ready for your next set of tests. I know that you saw Dr. Thomas recently, but he wanted me to schedule an appointment for you to come in for the next round."

"More tests?" I was expecting this call, but it's still surprising to actually have it happen. Every time I thought about what I would be doing when the doctor called, I pictured myself in my apron, cleaning up the kitchen after dinner, or lounging on the front porch, reading a good book.

I'm nervous, and I wipe my other hand on my jeans while I sit down on the edge of the garden bed.

"Yes, ma'am. The blood tests were only the beginning. We will do HLA typing, an MRI of your kidneys, a chest X-ray, and an EKG. Those are all pretty standard, but there are some others that Dr. Thomas may want to do as well, just to make sure that you're as healthy as possible and there won't be any problems. He wants to do them as close to the actual transplant date as possible just in case he finds any last-minute problems that pop up."

Oh. This is suddenly feeling more real than ever before. I knew this wasn't going to be a total cakewalk, but I thought I'd be getting through the tests a lot sooner than it seems like I'm going to. Seeing them written down on a piece of paper is one thing, but actually talking to the nurse about them all is another.

Still, it's all worth it just so I can help Kathleen. I'll be a little uncomfortable, but she's the one who might die without my help. Even though I'm a little worried about how painful this might all be, there's no way I'm backing out now.

"Are you still there?" She sounds a little worried that I might have hung up.

"Oh, yes. Sorry, I was thinking about when I'm going to be free to come to the office," I lie. Turning, I sit on the edge of the raised garden bed and stare up at the house. "How quickly can we get moving on this?"

"Dr. Thomas is pretty full this week." The receptionist sucks her teeth, and I hear her typing on the computer. "But what about Monday morning at eight? Would that be a good time for you to come in? You'll need to be fasting for a bit more blood work, but that way, you can get in and out and grab yourself some breakfast on the way home."

"Monday is great," I tell her, and I mean it.

Sure, it's a bit of a hassle, but knowing that Kathleen is going to be safe and healthy once she has my kidney will make all of this pain and testing worth it in the end. I know it will.

"Wonderful! I have you on the schedule. See you then!" She hangs up on me before I can respond, and I stand, slipping my phone into my pocket as I stare up at the house.

Scott and I bought this place fully intending to fill it every weekend with parties and friends. He wanted to entertain so he could rub elbows with people who might be able to help him in his career, and I loved the idea of being the young lawyer's wife.

We're not so young anymore, but that doesn't mean we can't still have parties and schmooze with people. A new sense of purpose rushes through me. I'm giving someone the gift of life, yet I'm not really living my own.

I'm going to plan a party, and Scott is going to be shocked. I can only imagine how excited he's going to be when he comes home from work and I have all of the plans in order for a nice party here on Saturday. It won't be a sit-down dinner, of course, because those have a lot of moving parts and will severely limit how many people you can actually have over, but I'm thinking of passed hors d'oeuvres, plenty of wine for people who can drink, and maybe even live music.

Hey, it's been a long time since we've entertained, so if we're going to do it, then we might as well go big. The weather this weekend is supposed to be perfect, so we could throw open the double doors that lead out to the back deck and have the musicians set up out there.

That way, people could flow through the house and even out into the yard if they want to.

I feel myself starting to get really excited. Parties are so much fun, and even though I'm not going to be able to drink,

I'll get to see everyone else enjoying themselves, and that's just as fun. There's no reason I can't enjoy myself and talk to some friends I haven't seen in a while.

Besides, the tests coming up on Monday don't sound very fun, so I figure I might as well enjoy myself while I can. It will be great to give Scott time to relax with friends from work, too. He's always saying how we need to invite some of his co-workers and their partners over for dinner, and I keep putting it off because I don't want to cook.

But a nice, big party like this? It's the perfect way to have everyone over at once, and nobody will expect me to be working in the kitchen the entire time with a huge guest list. This is the perfect win-win.

I debate for a moment whether I should call Scott and let him know what I'm doing or if I should just go ahead and start the planning. He's always telling me that I need to take more initiative in my life and live it a little, so I don't think I'm going to clue him in.

Won't he be surprised?

He won't see it coming.

A giggle escapes my lips, and I clap my hand over my mouth to stop it even though I'm the only person out here to hear me. Still, it's strange to giggle like a little kid.

I'm halfway to the house to start planning the menu for Saturday night when I'm hit by the best idea ever.

Everyone will be asking why I'm not drinking at the party, and I know it's going to get tiring to tell each and every person what's going on, so I'll just invite Kathleen. It'll be a great way for the two of us to spend a little bit more time together, and I honestly can't imagine that she won't appreciate it.

Who wouldn't want to go to a party? And I'm sorry, but I doubt that she's ever been to a party like the ones I throw.

Now I'm giddy, and I giggle again as I hurry into the house. There's a lot to do, a lot of moving pieces to put together, and I need to get started. This is going to be amazing.

Kathleen's going to love it, I just know it.

18

SCOTT

I almost don't want to come home because I already know what Erin is up to, and it's fun to watch her be excited through the cameras I have set up in the house. It's not that I don't want to spend time with my wife, but I really just love watching her be so excited as she buzzes around. I always check in on her before heading home, and I was surprised to see her scurrying to and fro, making sure that the house is even more picked up than usual. I knew right away what she was planning.

What I don't quite know yet is why she's doing it right now.

I know she's a little stressed out about all the tests that she's going to have to endure to be a donor. If she weren't stressed, then I'd be worried about her and wonder if she was thinking this all the way through. Besides being there to support her, there's really nothing I can do to take away her stress.

I'm encouraging her all that I can without coming across as too pushy. There's a lot at stake here, but she has no idea just how much we could both lose if she doesn't go through with the transplant. The last thing I want to do is push her too hard and make her wonder why I'm being overly supportive. It's a fine balance, but I'm sure I can walk it.

In addition to her being stressed, I also know that she went to meet Kathleen at the bar where she works. Of course Erin would want to make sure that the woman is kind and deserves a kidney, but even if she were a horrible person, my wife would probably still be willing to get on the operating table.

She's just that good, through and through. Not me, though. I know that people aren't always good, and I refuse to let my family be hurt because of that. In this world, you either take what you need to survive and to protect the people you love, or someone takes it from you.

The kitchen lights are dimmed when I walk into the house, and I set my briefcase down before calling for Erin. When she doesn't answer, I walk through the house to the back deck, where she's dragging the furniture around to make space for a band.

Because, yes, of course she's going to have live music at this thing on Saturday. I can only imagine how much this is all going to cost us, but it really doesn't matter.

"Hey, darling," I say, coming up behind her to give her a kiss. She turns in my arms and hugs me, leaning up to press her lips against mine. I'm suddenly filled with the thoughts of what else we could be doing right now, but before my mind can wander too far down that path, she pulls back and swings her arms out to show me what she's done.

"What do you think?"

I eyeball it. All the tables and chairs have been pushed over to one side of the deck. The grill's been moved from where it's stood since we moved in and is now up next to the house. Even though I know exactly what she's doing, I can't let on about that yet. She can't ever know that I watch her when she's at home. "You're nesting?"

She laughs. "I'm getting ready for a party on Saturday! Doesn't that sound fun?" Her excitement is contagious, and she continues talking before I have a chance to respond to her question. "I've already got the caterer and the live music ready to go. The guest list is on the kitchen table for you to look at, but I've already started calling around and getting people on board to come. What do you think?"

"I think you're incredible," I tell her, pulling her into my arms so that I can kiss her. My arms wrap all the way around her, she's so thin. When she leans against my chest, I rub her back. "I can't believe that you have the mental space to put something like this together when I know you have to be thinking about the donation almost every waking second."

She shrugs, letting my concerns roll off her back. "You always worry about me," she says, going up on her tiptoes to give me a kiss. "But you don't need to because I really want to do this, Scott. It's nice to have something to think about rather than just sitting around waiting for my next doctor's appointment. Oh! I didn't tell you the best part. I invited Kathleen."

Kathleen? I must have missed this little tidbit of information when I was checking in on her throughout the day. "Kathleen? The woman you're giving your kidney to? What makes you want to do that?"

She shrugs and snuggles into my chest. "You haven't met her, Scott. I don't want to come across like I pity her, because that's not kind, but she's definitely had a really hard life, and it's not fair to her that she has to deal with the cards she's been dealt. Also, I know that this is probably dumb, but I feel drawn to help her. It's like she's more than just someone I'm giving a kidney to. It's like she's family."

I exhale hard. This was not what I was expecting when I

figured out that Erin was busy planning a party today. The one thing I have to make sure of is that nobody at the party says or does something that will discourage Erin from going through with the donation. That's why I have to choose my next words very carefully so that I don't accidentally upset my wife.

"I think that's about the kindest thing you could do for her, but I want you to really think about it before you invite her. Erin, you told me how she dresses. Do you really think she'd feel comfortable here?"

Erin stares at me like she can't quite believe what I'm saying. "You do pro bono work," she points out. "You know how important it is not to judge people by what they look like or what they can afford."

"I'm not going to be judging her, and I know you certainly wouldn't. I'm just worried what some of the other people here would say and if she'll feel out of place." Erin has pulled out of my arms, and I take a step back, holding mine out from my body to show her that I'm not a threat. "I think that if you want to do this, you have to make sure she's going to feel comfortable and have as much fun as you are."

"You're not saying this because you're uncomfortable with having her here?"

"What? No." I sigh, rolling my neck and reaching up to rub it while I think of how to make my point without coming across like a jerk. "Erin, I don't want her to feel uncomfortable, but I also don't want our friends to feel uncomfortable. Listen, you can invite her, but make sure that she knows what she's getting into."

Her jaw hangs open slightly, and I know she's really frustrated with me, but I need to make her see how important it is that this doesn't all fall to pieces. It's one thing for her to plan a party without cluing me in on it before she gets started, but another thing entirely to throw a party that may make her decide to back out on the donation.

I know how some of the guys I work with can be, and I also know that their wives would never willingly donate a kidney to someone, family or not. I can't have those people whispering in her ear all night long and planting seeds of doubt.

"You're a jerk. I want to do something really nice for this woman, and you—"

"I'm not telling you not to be nice! You're giving her your kidney!" Her eyes go wide at the tone of my voice, and I stop to take a deep breath. "I'm sorry. I just want you to see how important it is that you're careful, okay? You know that some of our friends won't be as supportive about your going through with this, and I don't want them to sway you when you want to do it so badly."

"That's really the only problem?"

"Of course it is." I take her hand in mine and rub my thumb across her knuckles. "You have the kindest heart, Erin. You are thoughtful and giving, but the rest of the world isn't necessarily like that. I don't want someone to make you think you're doing the wrong thing because they don't understand it."

She melts. Of course she does. If there's one thing I know about my wife, it's how to make her relax and trust me. If she didn't trust me, then she'd ask questions about why she never gets to see the reports from her doctor or why I haven't ever encouraged her to work outside the house or make close friends.

"Thank you," she tells me, reaching up to cup my cheek. "Seriously, Scott, for everything. For supporting me in this decision and looking out for me. But you don't have to worry. I promised Kathleen that I wouldn't back out of the donation, and some snarky remarks at a party aren't going to change my mind, okay?"

"As long as you're sure. There's no reason we can't hire musicians for just the two of us to enjoy."

Her laugh fills the backyard, and I feel my heart squeeze. She really has no idea how much I love her, how much I miss her when we're apart.

Hell, I don't know many husbands who would be willing to go as far as I am to make sure that their spouse is healthy.

I found my wife a kidney and am willing to pay whatever it takes to get it. How many husbands can say they love their wives that much?

19

KATHLEEN

The dress I'm wearing fits me better than anything I've ever had on in my life and clings to me like it was made for my body. When I move, it moves with me, shining and sparkling thanks to the sequins sewn all over it. Even though it's just long enough to barely touch the floor, I have on shoes that are strappy and sleek and that perfectly match the dress so it won't drag while I walk.

"It's too much," I say, turning to look at Erin. She's standing behind me with her hands clasped in front of her, grinning at me like she's never been prouder of a person. "Seriously, Erin, this is lovely, but it's too much."

And I don't just mean in general. The price tag sticks straight out from under my arm, and I couldn't help but catch sight of the price scrawled on the tag when I was being helped into the dress.

Because apparently, when you have a lot of money, not only is it not a big deal to drop three hundred dollars on a dress, but the staff at the store will also get into the fitting room with you to help you put it on.

"It's perfect," Erin says, more to the woman standing next

to me, looking at my reflection in the mirror, than to me. "We'll take it. And the shoes, of course."

The woman gives Erin a little nod and a smile and then disappears from the back fitting area, probably to go ring up the purchase and gloat that she just managed the easiest sale of the day.

"Erin," I say, but she doesn't let me finish.

"Nope. Kathleen, this is on me, okay? You don't need to worry about a thing. I want to have you over on Saturday for our party, but if the only reason you won't come is because you don't have an outfit to wear, then this will take care of that, okay? Please let me buy it for you. Please come to my house."

I don't know what to say, so instead I give her one jerky nod. Never in my life have I had someone so willing to take care of me like this. Sure, my parents probably would have loved to be able to take me shopping and buy me nice clothes at the mall instead of relying on hand-me-downs, but the money just wasn't there.

Not like this. Not in the way it is for Erin, like there's more in her account than she knows what to do with, and she is willing to spend it on anyone who asks.

Or who looks like they need new clothes.

I certainly didn't ask for a new dress and shoes, but I have to admit that I like it. I like her taking care of me even though I know it's all going to come to an end soon. After the kidney donation, there's no way I'll ever see her again.

So why not take advantage of it now?

The thought passes through my mind before I can stop it, and I try to push it away, but it's already settled there like it's going to hibernate. I feel it resonate through my head, and it must show on my face because Erin walks up to me, puts her hand on my shoulder, and gives it a squeeze.

"Is there anything else you need while we're at the mall? I

love shopping and don't really have a friend to shop with, so you just tell me if there's anything else you want. My treat. I'm serious."

Is this for real? I look at her, trying to really read her face, but she's staring at me with an open and honest expression, and I can't believe it. Nobody is this nice, especially not to a person they just met, but she seems willing to swipe her credit card and buy me whatever I want.

"I really can't," I say, but she laughs.

"But I can! And what about your daughter? How old is she? I bet she'd like some new clothes, wouldn't she?"

Cora would love nothing more. I can only imagine the look on her face if I were to tell her that this woman wants to buy the two of us whatever we both want from the mall. It's impossible to believe, but maybe, just maybe, Erin is telling the truth. I guess there's only one way to find out.

"She's fourteen, and she does need new shoes," I admit. I don't even have to pretend to be a little embarrassed by this because it kills me that I'm not able to get my daughter exactly what she needs. "I hate to ask you, but her feet have grown a lot this year, and I just haven't been able to take her to get new ones. I know it sounds whiny, but every penny I make goes right into the fund for my transplant."

That is the truth. All of it. Cora needs new shoes, I can't buy them for her, and all the money I have goes into savings so I can afford the necessary surgery. Cora's sick all the time, even though it makes her angry to admit it, and I'm constantly having to worry about paying her doctor's bills.

Making her sick is the only way I can convince her that she needs the transplant. I'm still not quite sure that she believes me, and I'm starting to think I'm going to have to work harder to make my point clear.

Cora is sick. Or she has to be, if I'm going to pull this entire thing off.

Luckily, Dr. Thomas is really good to us and willing to write off most of the treatment she needs, but I know it's only going to get worse after the transplant with the aftercare and appointments. Cora doesn't always look sick, which is why she doesn't believe that she is, but I know the truth.

Mothers always know the truth, and we always know what's best.

"Then we're getting her new shoes," Erin declares, "but after you change. Need help with the dress?" Her fingers are right by the zipper like she can't wait to unzip it and help me out, but I shake my head, hurrying away from her to the fitting room.

"I'm fine," I call. "Don't worry about me." My fingers tremble a little bit as I undo the zipper and let the dress fall to the floor. When I step out of the shoes, I'm careful not to accidentally step on the fabric.

Turning in front of the mirror, I trace my finger over the scar that curves right along the inside of my hip.

"Are you stuck?" Erin's right outside the dressing room, and I watch in horror as the door jiggles in the frame.

"I'm fine!" Hurrying, I grab the shirt that I wore in and yank it down over my head. My heart slams in my chest as I pull my jeans on and zip them up. "Seriously, I'm good. Just didn't want to break the zipper!"

The fitting room door swings open, and Erin stands there, a concerned look on her face. "Did you think it was going to break? We can ask for a different dress if it feels a little weak. The last thing I want to do is buy you something that isn't great quality."

"It's fine." Bending, I scoop up the dress and the shoes and walk past Erin. My heart is still hammering in my chest.

I'm not good at pretending to be someone or something that I'm not, and these clothes, this shopping trip, even the upcoming party are all so far out of my comfort zone that it would be laughable if it weren't so uncomfortable.

"Great." Erin either doesn't pick up on the fact that I'm uncomfortable or she doesn't seem to care. Walking next to me, she slips her arm through mine and leads me up to the checkout. "I really can't wait to go shopping with you! I'm sure you know your daughter's size, and anything you see that she wants, I'm happy to get it for her. I can only imagine how scared she must be with all your health problems."

"She's a really good girl," I say, choosing my words carefully. Erin might not be the brightest crayon in the box, but there's no reason I should give her more information than she really needs. "I'm sure she'll appreciate this more than you'll ever know."

"Whatever she needs," Erin says, grinning at me as she hands her credit card over to the clerk. "Seriously, Kathleen, whatever she needs. You tell me what it is, and I'll make it happen."

She has no idea just how true that is.

I t's just a few minutes before the party is supposed to get started. Outside on the back deck, I can hear the string quartet warming up. They sound discordant now, but judging by the sample of music I heard on their website, they're going to sound amazing as soon as they're all playing together.

The food smells delicious and is all plated and ready to be passed. I hired a caterer, and they put together a tasting menu with six different main options, three soups in little shooter glasses, and even a few different types of dessert that they'll pass around as the night goes on.

Of course, hiring a caterer means that I'm kicked out of the kitchen for now, but that's fine with me. I'd much rather be dressed to the nines, sipping sparkling apple juice, and talking with friends than worrying about making sure there's enough cheesecake to go around.

The waitstaff are all standing by the kitchen. There are three of them, dressed in matching black and white outfits, ready to serve.

"You look incredible," Scott says, coming down the stairs

and walking up behind me. "How in the world did I get so lucky that you're smart, funny, can plan a party, and are gorgeous?"

Laughing, I turn and lean against him. "Thanks for letting me do this," I say, giving him a hug. "I think it'll be a lot of fun."

"It's all you." He pulls back from me when the doorbell rings. "Would you like to do the honors?"

I can't help but grin at him before going over to open the front door. Some of the people I invited I only know by name and haven't ever met them, but it's easy to see that nobody standing on our front porch is lost. Everyone is dressed to the nines in gorgeous dresses and suits that probably cost more than most people pay for their car payment each month.

There's a dozen people on the porch, all of them probably having walked up from the side driveway together, and in the back I see Kathleen. "Come on in, everyone," I say, putting on my hostess smile. The music rises behind me, and I fling the front doors open wide. "I'm so glad you all could make it."

Couples file in, the women stopping to talk to me. I smile at Scott's partner, Alexander Parks, and his wife, Monica. She's absolutely dripping with diamonds, which makes her look more like she's on her way to a movie premiere than to dinner at my house, but I don't care.

I'm just glad everyone made it. I want us all to have a great time and for Kathleen to really enjoy herself. She hangs back, watching as I greet everyone, then finally makes her way to the door, moving slowly and carefully like she's afraid she's going to turn an ankle in her new shoes.

"You look amazing," I tell her, drawing her into a hug. "I'm so glad you made it."

She pulls back, and I think I see a flash of nervousness cross her face, but she smiles, and it disappears. "I don't really think I fit in here," she tells me, but I'm already shaking my head.

"Don't you worry about that." Just like when we were at the store, shopping for clothes, we link arms, and I lead her into the house. Everything is perfect. The food. The music. The guests. I can't wait for everyone here to see her and learn who she is.

I don't know exactly how it happened, but I feel like I've taken Kathleen under my wing. I want to show her how amazing life can be and that there are kind people in the world who are in her corner. Sure, some of the guests here can be a little bit rough around the edges, but I have no doubt that everyone will be wonderful to her when they learn about her story.

Stopping a waiter as he walks by, I grab us each a glass of bubbly apple juice. There's plenty of champagne and wine for the other guests, but I gave the caterer strict instructions that we needed to be able to get our hands on a nonalcoholic drink whenever we wanted one.

"This is the house," I tell her, leading her through to the backyard. "And you're welcome to come inside if you get chilled, but I think most of the party will be outside. That's where the musicians are set up, and people tend to gravitate to the live music."

"That's not a CD?" She sounds surprised, and I squeeze her arm.

"No, I wanted tonight to be really nice, so I thought I'd go ahead and hire in some strings. They're nice, aren't they?" This is my world, and I'm giddy with the fact that I get to share it with Kathleen. I can't imagine never having been part of this world before, but this is all new to her, and it's my job to show her around.

We step out onto the deck, and she gasps. It's still early enough that there's a little natural light out from the sun, but the hard work I put into making this look amazing is obvious. There are fairy lights strung up around the deck as well as some solar lights out in the yard. With the string music playing from a dark corner of the deck and gorgeous lights glowing around us, it looks magical.

"This is amazing," she says, then shakes her head. "You really didn't have to invite me here, Erin. Seriously. I don't want to be in the way of your friends."

"Oh, stop." Pulling her, I drag her over to where Scott is talking with Alexander and Monica. My husband pauses in the conversation when we walk up, his eyes flicking over Kathleen before he looks at me.

"You must be Kathleen," he says, holding his hand out to her. "Welcome to our home. I'm so glad you came tonight."

"It's gorgeous," she tells him, her eyes locked on his. "Thanks for having me."

"I'm Monica." The woman across from me inserts herself in the conversation. "Now, have we met? How do you know Erin?"

Silence descends on us like darkness at sunset as Scott, Kathleen, and I all think of how to best answer her question. I'm dying to tell everyone here how I know Kathleen, but the last thing I want to do is embarrass the poor woman.

Luckily, she clears her throat. "Erin is actually giving me a kidney," she says, her cheeks flushing. Looking at her, you might think that she'd had some alcohol to drink that caused the flush, but I know for a fact that I gave her apple juice. She must be terribly embarrassed, so I speak up, wanting to smooth things over the best I can.

"It's nothing. Kathleen is amazing. Believe me, you guys will love her. If giving her a kidney is the best way for me to help her, then I'm going to do it."

"That's so kind of you," Monica coos, her attention now fully on my face. "So unselfish. So you two don't really know each other?" She flicks her finger back and forth between the two of us, and I shake my head.

"Not really, but we're becoming good friends."

"Amazing." Alexander's staring at the two of us like he's never seen anything more interesting in his life. "Did you have a billboard, Kathleen? I think I recall seeing one on my way out of town."

There's the flush again, only now it's deeper. This is not going the way I thought it would, and I want to smooth it over, but she nods bravely and does her best to smile at him.

"That wasn't me," she says. "But there are so many people on the waiting list for a kidney that sometimes you have to think outside the box."

"Smart." Scott speaks up, surprising me. "You know, I read a piece in the paper the other day about the organ black market that goes on. Not so much here, of course, but in other countries. It's terrible, what they're being forced to go through."

"People are selling their organs?" Monica looks shocked, and I'm sure I know why. She's so used to having money that it wouldn't ever cross her mind that she'd have to sell anything to get what she wanted. "Why on earth would they do that?"

"They need money," Kathleen confirms with a nod. "It's scary, but Scott is right. Doctors will tell patients that they can make a quick buck, but then they don't tell them about all of the risks and steps they'll have to go through before donation."

"And you know all of what you'll have to do?" Alexander pins his gaze on me, and I suddenly feel like I'm on the stand. "You've had everything explained to you so that you know what you're getting yourself into?"

I nod, trying to look as confident as possible, completely aware of how everyone is looking at me. Scott beams at me like he couldn't be prouder, and Kathleen is staring at me with adoration. I'm doing my best to keep any doubts from showing on my face, but each appointment with Dr. Thomas involves new tests and blood work, and I'm getting a little tired of being a human pincushion. It's not like I could ever back out now, no matter how nervous I feel. This is what I signed up for.

"Erin's ready," Kathleen says with just as much confidence as I'm feeling right now. "She wouldn't back out on me, would you?"

Everyone is waiting for me to answer. I know it's ridiculous, but it honestly feels like all the people at the party, even the musicians, are looking at me and waiting to hear what I'm going to say. Even Scott can't seem to stop smiling and looking at me.

He and I have talked about this a thousand times, it seems, but it's obvious that he, and everyone else, wants to hear my answer.

"I wouldn't dare," I say, turning to loop my arm around Kathleen's waist and pull her to me. "I want to do this, and there's nothing that will stop me."

Before Monica or Alexander can say anything, Scott reaches out and touches my shoulder. "You two know my wife. She's the most thoughtful person I know. I'm so proud of her for making this decision."

He beams at me, but that doesn't stop the whisper of doubt that I feel in the back of my head. It's only growing there because of what Alexander and Monica said, I know that, but it's still there, and I have to make it shut up.

Donating my kidney to Kathleen seemed like an incredible idea. It still is, right? Then why do I feel a sense of unease creep up my spine? I know I tend to jump into situations without really looking at all the moving pieces, but it's never been a problem before.

Kathleen squeezes my arm and gives me a little nod and smile.

Look at her. She needs me. I might be scared, but that doesn't mean I have the right to back out of helping her, right? That's not who I am. I'm not the type of person to offer to help and then back out at the last second. I give my head a little shake to clear it from the nasty thoughts that Monica and her husband placed there.

Besides, Kathleen looks close to the edge. I can only imagine what she'd do if yet another person offered to help her and then didn't go through with it.

21

KATHLEEN

I thought for sure that Erin was going to back out on me last night at the party, and I'm not entirely sure how I would have handled it if she had. It's not like I could have argued with her, not with all her friends right there and her husband standing at her side. I'm sure of how that would have looked.

The poor woman who needs a kidney falling apart at a dinner party where she most definitely doesn't fit in isn't a good look for anyone.

"You're in a foul mood," my mother says, coming into the kitchen, where I'm pushing down some Pop-Tarts in the toaster. "Didn't enjoy dressing up and pretending to be Cinderella last night, huh?"

"It was fine." I grit my teeth and turn away from her. The last thing I want to do is admit to her how frustrating the night was. I'm sure that most people would have killed to get an invitation to that dinner party, but I felt terribly out of place.

Not only that, but I saw the look that crossed Erin's face

when that nosy lawyer and his wife pushed her on whether she was really ready to donate her kidney.

It was doubt, just a flash of it, there and gone before anyone else even noticed it. Even Scott, who dotes on Erin and treats her like she walks on water, didn't see the flash of it appear on her face, I'm sure of it.

But I know that look. I've seen it on people's faces dozens of times before. Even Erin, who talks a big game of being willing to bend over backward for someone she doesn't know, suddenly had a flash of doubt about whether what she's doing is a good idea.

"Fine? You looked like you were going to a movie premiere. Tell me, did the rich people not make you feel welcome?"

The toaster pops, and I grab the food, ignoring the way it burns my fingers. Tossing them onto two plates, I hold them out in front of my body like a shield when I turn to look at her. "They were lovely."

"But something happened." One of these plates is for Cora, and my mom knows it, but she still takes it from me. I don't have the energy to try to stop her, which means that I'll just have to give my daughter this one and get something else for myself. "What was it, Kathleen? You act like you can hide it, but your face is a dead giveaway that there was a problem."

Is it, now? If that's the truth, then that's something I'm definitely going to have to work on.

Before I can say anything, my mom speaks again. "You think she's going to back out, don't you? I can tell from the look on your face."

"No." I shake my head, although I'm not sure that I'm going to be able to convince either of us. "It's not that. She wouldn't do that."

"Are you sure?" She's holding her food, about to take a bite, but now she drops it back down to the plate and stares at me. "I thought Dr. Thomas promised you that she was good for the kidneys. What in the world are you going to do if you need to restart this process with someone else? The tests are all going well, the blood work is good . . . and the doctor said you don't have a lot more time."

"I know that!" Turning, I slam the plate down hard on the counter. It cracks in two, the pieces falling apart from each other, but I don't worry about that right now. I'm more focused on the woman standing there in front of me. It feels like she's baiting me.

"Then what are you going to do? If she backs out, then where does that leave you? Where does that leave Cora? If she needs help, what will you do? Are you sure this is the right thing to do?" Each word is carefully selected and feels like a knife.

She's cutting straight into me. My mom knew that her words would hurt, which was why she chose them. She knew that bringing my daughter into the conversation would be more than enough to really get my attention.

"I'm going to take care of it," I promise her, then pull my phone from my pocket and check the time. Ten in the morning. It is Sunday, but I don't think Scott and Erin go to church. He might be hurting this morning—I saw him drink more than his fair share of beer last night—but she and I abstained so that we could go through with the transplant.

"Fix this," my mother hisses as I stalk from the room. "Do you really think you're going to be able to find another person who would be such a good match?"

I ignore her as I walk out of the kitchen and onto the front porch. Our house is nothing like Erin's. There's no impressive landscaping, no huge wraparound deck for entertaining, just a wonky front porch with boards that need to be replaced and a spotty yard with scrub grass.

Still, I think better outside than in, and this is where I

want to stand while I make this call. Mentally, I cross my fingers and prepare myself for how this conversation will go. I need to see Erin. Need to get her out of her house and out of her head so that I can make sure she's still going to help me out.

She picks up on the first ring, just like I hoped she would. That was the easy part. The difficult part is going to be making sure that she will come out with me and isn't going to turn me down when I tell her I need to see her.

"Hey, Erin," I say, making sure that my voice is as light and happy as possible. "How are you this morning? I wanted to call and tell you what a wonderful time I had last night!"

"Thank you, you're sweet." She sounds tired and pauses a moment before speaking again. The whole time she's silent, though, I feel my heart beating hard in my chest, and all I can do is hope she isn't going to back out on me now. "It was a good time, wasn't it? Scott and I are so glad you were able to make it."

She and Scott may have been happy that I showed up, but I highly doubt that some of their rich friends were thrilled to see me there. Instead of mentioning that, however, I turn the conversation back around to the two of us. "I was hoping you could talk me through planning a party like that," I tell her, even though there's no way I'd ever throw an event like she did. "It's a really nice day out, and I thought we could go to the park, sit under the pavilion, even each bring a small picnic. What do you think?"

She's silent, and I know she's trying to decide just how to let me down as easily as possible. I'm sure Scott wants to see her today, or at least will want her to decrease the amount of time that the two of us are spending together, but that's simply something I can't let happen.

"I'm sure you're exhausted from last night, and what I make won't be nearly as good as the caterer," I continue, laying it on thickly, "but I really would love to see you and thank you for having me. It was such a treat. You're an incredible friend."

There. Erin is one of the nicest people I've ever met, and if that doesn't inspire her to meet me at the park even though she doesn't really want to, then I don't know what will.

"That sounds amazing," she tells me. "I have tons of cheesecake left over from last night, so I'll bring that if you'd like."

"Perfect." I punch the air, a huge grin spreading across my face. "See you there at noon?"

That gives me about three hours to make something for lunch and to get to the park. It's plenty long enough for me to do what needs to be done, but hopefully not so long that Erin will have time to back out.

"Noon is great. See you then." Her voice is still cheery, but when I hang up the phone, I feel a pit in my stomach.

She's in her head. Her rich friends got into her mind last night and planted seeds of doubt there, which is absolutely the last thing I need from her. I need her head fully in the game. I need her willing to do whatever it takes to make this kidney transplant happen.

Turning, I look back at the house. Cora is probably in her room, listening to music. That seems to be all she wants to do recently since I won't let her go out with friends anymore. I know she'd love to, but she's just so fragile.

Just because she doesn't feel sick right now doesn't mean she isn't. That's what I've tried to explain to her time and time again. That's what I've tried to get her to understand, tried to get Dr. Thomas to make clear to her.

That's why I started making her sick myself so she would finally listen to me. It was easy enough to get my hands on disulfiram to give Cora and easier still to mix some high-proof vodka into her juice at night when she thinks she's healthier than she is.

It's not enough vodka to make her drunk, just enough to make her terribly sick.

She wants to live a long and healthy life? Then she needs to be more respectful and let me take care of her. I know what it's like to live with a kidney that won't pull its weight and how terrible it is to have to wait on a list that only seems to grow longer.

I'm not going to let that happen to her.

No matter what I have to do.

22

ERIN

I don't like the nerves that eat at me when I pull up to the park right before noon. This isn't a big deal—it's just lunch with Kathleen so she can thank me for having her over for the dinner party last night. She'd seemed so out of place at times, like a fish out of water, but she never said anything about being uncomfortable, and I just assumed that she was a little awkward in social situations.

Shaking my head to clear it, I try to pull my mind back to what I'm doing right now and not focus on what happened last night. I honestly thought it would be a great chance for everyone to get to meet her and to see what I'm doing for her. I loved the idea of my friends all learning about my upcoming donation and supporting her.

But they weren't all on board. I remember the look of shock on Alexander's face when we told him what was going on. He'd been . . . *appalled*, I guess, is the right word.

And that's not good because he's always whispering in Scott's ear. The two of them are inseparable at work, always taking on huge clients together, always staying late at the office to make sure that loose ends are all tied up neatly in a bow. For the longest time, I used to joke that Alexander was Scott's work wife, but I stopped joking about that a while ago when it felt a little bit too true.

Then again, Scott was supportive last night. He stood up for me and told Alexander and Monica how proud he is of me for donating my kidney to Kathleen. But what if he changes his mind? What if he tries to stop me?

My palms grow sweaty, and I wipe them on my jeans. I need to stop thinking about that right now, especially because I know that Kathleen is probably waiting for me.

Pressing my key fob to lock my car, I pick up the tray of cheesecake and carry it over to the pavilion. Kathleen was dying to meet me for lunch today, and I know I should be grateful that she wants to return the favor of a nice meal, but I wish she didn't feel like she has to do this to return the favor.

That's terrible of me, and I know it, but after last night, I want to take some time to myself to really think about what I'm doing.

There. I said it. That's a terrible thing to think, especially when I know she's been through so many potential donors who have backed out after getting her hopes up. I promised her and myself that I wouldn't do that, but now I'm beginning to wonder if I'm making a mistake.

I'm not. I know I'm not. It's just . . . this all started last night.

It's all because of Alexander, I know it. He's the first person to express any doubt about the donation, so why am I listening to him? Probably because one thing that I read online was how important it was to have supportive people around you before you go through with the surgery.

What if he gets into Scott's head? The last thing I need is my husband telling me that I'm making a terrible decision by trying to help Kathleen.

My feet seem to grow heavier and heavier as I draw closer

to the pavilion. A strong burst of wind blows through the park, and I turn to watch some little kids playing on the playground. It's been forever since I came to this park, mostly because seeing mothers with little kids was just too painful for me.

Stopping, I raise my hand to shield my eyes and look for my friend. I may not be able to come here with my biological children, but Kathleen needs me the same way they would. I know that she's not my child, not related to me at all, but I can't help but feel that same type of affinity for her, so I do my best to push any doubts I have about the donation from my mind.

When I see Kathleen sitting under the pavilion, I start in her direction. She's waving at me, her arm way up above her head to get my attention, a huge smile on her face.

She looks so different from last night that I'm sure if anyone from the party were to see her, they'd walk right on by without recognizing her. The gorgeous dress and the shoes that made her look like she'd had a butt lift are gone. Even from here, I can see that she's wearing jeans and old sneakers as well as a light sweater that looks like it's seen better days.

"Erin!" Now she's standing and waving harder like she's not sure if she's gotten my attention, so I turn to her, throwing her a quick wave before hurrying under the pavilion to join her.

"Kathleen, hey," I say, sitting down across from her. "Thanks so much for the lunch invite."

She reaches across the table and squeezes my hand. "Seriously, I know that this won't come anywhere near thanking you for last night and what you've done for me—what you're doing for me—but I wanted to spend some time with you. And I figured you didn't want to cook lunch, so I'd make it for us! Besides that, I wanted to thank you for buying everything for Cora. She was thrilled, as you can probably imagine."

"Was she? Good." I smile at my friend. "I'm so glad she liked everything."

"She really did." Kathleen sighs. "Fourteen is a rough age, but she's a really good kid. Anyway, I hope you enjoy the break from having to cook."

I don't have the heart to tell her that my refrigerator is stuffed with leftovers, so, for the first time in a while, I'm not going to have to lie to Scott about where our meals are coming from. "You nailed it," I tell her, pushing the cheesecake to the side. "And I brought plenty of dessert."

She grins and unpacks a cardboard box that's on the bench next to her. "I need to get to the store this week, but I've been feeling a little run-down," she tells me, giving me a grimace and touching her side. "Kidney stuff, you know."

I nod. "Does it make you feel tired all the time?"

She sighs. "Yeah, pretty much. Once I get the new one from you, I'll be better than ever, according to Dr. Thomas. Oh, speaking of which, I had a message from him this morning. He wants to set a date for the transplant. Probably in a few days, hopefully. It depends on how things go, but he wants to move on this as soon as possible."

A few days. That's so soon. "I had no idea we'd be able to do it that quickly," I tell her. "It really feels like we just got started on the tests. And what in the world is he doing working on the weekend?" I try to keep my voice light to hide some of the worry that springs up in me.

She shrugs, but the look on her face is anything but casual. "He's devoted to his patients and takes this seriously. But does that not work for you?" She sounds concerned, and when I glance up at her, I'm not surprised to see her frowning a little bit. "Do you have something big going on that we need to work around?"

"Nothing like that." I grin at her, trying to make myself look as happy and unconcerned as possible even though deep down in my heart, I'm replaying a conversation with Monica from last night.

She'd wanted to know how well I really know *the woman*, if I was sure I could trust her.

I'd laughed at her. Why in the world would Kathleen pretend that she needed a new kidney if she didn't? It's absurd. Still, the doubt on Monica's face soured the evening. Why can't people just see that this is something I want to do because it's the right thing?

I'm sure that if Scott had heard what Monica was saying, he would have defended my decision, but he and Alexander were off in a corner of the deck together, whispering about a case they're working on.

"Are you changing your mind?" Kathleen sucks in a breath like she's trying to keep from crying, and that sound makes me look up at her. "Oh, God, you are."

"No!" This time, it's my turn to reach across the table and take her hand. "No, I'm not, Kathleen, okay? I promise you, I wouldn't do that to you. I'm just surprised at how fast it's all happening, that's all."

"Not for me." She shakes her head. "It's not happening fast for me. This has been something I've been fighting for years, and I thought I finally saw the light at the end of the tunnel."

Tears fill her eyes, and she moves to pull her hand back from me, but I don't let her go. Regret pours through me, and I suddenly feel overwhelmed.

I'm the reason she feels so terrible right now. Here she is, a sweet and sick lady, who just wanted to invite me out to a picnic to thank me for my kindness, and I'm making her cry.

"Kathleen," I say, but she shakes her head.

"I'm sorry. I shouldn't cry. It's just that . . . wow. I'm sorry." She sucks in a breath and looks at a point over my head for a moment before locking her eyes back on mine. "I know it's stupid, but if there's any chance of my having your organ and it keeping me alive, then there's no reason not to be honest with you."

"You can be honest with me," I tell her. "Of course you can."

"I thought that I might have not only found someone who would give me an organ, but also a friend." Her eyes are watery, and when she blinks, two fat tears roll down her thin cheeks. "We're so different, we both see that, but that doesn't mean we can't be friends, and I thought that might be what was happening."

It feels like someone just punched me in the chest. Sucking in a gasp, I brace my elbow on the table and lean my chin on my hand. How could I be so blind to this poor woman? There I was last night, dressed in a gown and jewelry that probably cost more than her mortgage every month, and I didn't see how much pain she was in.

All I could see was how important it was to me to impress my rich friends and for them to like her. They looked sideways at her, we both know that, and I allowed what they hissed in my ear to affect how I was going to act.

Now I feel terrible. I shouldn't have let them get into my head like that. That's all Alexander and Monica were doing—getting into my head. I don't know why they'd do that, not when they act like we're all such good friends, but that's all it was.

And I let them do it.

"Kathleen," I tell her, looking her dead in the eyes so I can try to make my point as clear as possible, "you don't need to worry about me, okay? I want to help you. I'm really sorry if last night was uncomfortable for you at all or if you felt like you didn't belong, but I swear to you, that's over now, okay? I'm going to do whatever it takes to help you."

For a moment, she doesn't answer. Then she exhales hard,

like she was holding her breath and hoping I was going to say just that. "Are you sure? You're really one hundred percent in, no matter what?"

There's a small voice in the back of my head wondering why she puts it like that, but I push it away. She's scared and looking for whatever reassurance I can give her, and I'm going to give it to her.

"No matter what."

She smiles now, a secret smile like the one you would share with a friend and nobody else. "No matter what."

23

Erin came home from her picnic with Kathleen looking a little worse for wear. Normally, I might not notice things like this, especially on a Sunday when I need to be preparing for my next big case, but I saw the way she slipped quietly into the house, noticed how she barely spoke to me, then watched her as she went outside to sit in the sun.

That's not typical for my wife. Normally, I can expect a blow-by-blow story of what she was just up to, but she doesn't seem in the mood to talk. Standing in the living room, I watch her, and I'm torn.

I should go out there to see if she's okay, but I also have to prepare for court tomorrow.

Alexander and I are working on a case together, and I'm sure he's going to spend his entire Sunday afternoon preparing. He's not the type of man to do anything casually, and Monica will probably be off with her friends, playing tennis or getting highlights, so that she isn't in the house to bother him.

As much as I'd like to lock myself in my home office to

work on this case, it's obvious that something is really bothering Erin, and I need to figure out what it is. The last thing I need is for her to have second thoughts about the donation.

I've done everything I can to set it up and make sure that she goes through with it. If someone made her question her decision last night, then I need to put a stop to it and get her back on board.

I have a pretty good feeling that she's upset about how last night with her friend went. Monica wasn't exactly supportive of her idea to donate a kidney, and while I know that shouldn't matter to me or to my wife, I saw the expression on her face.

Both she and her husband think it's stupid. They think that putting anyone else's needs above your own at the risk of hurting yourself is a terrible idea, and the more he droned on about it after Erin and Kathleen had left our little group to get something to eat, the more nervous I got.

I'm sure Monica did her best to get in Erin's head, and I have to do whatever it takes to get my wife back in the game.

Straightening my shoulders, I walk not into my office, like I'd prefer, but outside to see if I can talk some sense into my wife. Preparing for my case is important, but nothing is more important than making sure that Erin is still willing to go through with the surgery.

My shadow falls on her when I walk up to her. She's stretched out on her favorite zero-gravity chair, relaxing in the sun like a cat, and she blinks up at me when I block her rays.

"I thought you'd be working by now," she tells me, sitting up. The chair moves with her, and she locks it into its new position so she can look at me without staring right up at my face. "Is something wrong? Anything you need me to do for you?"

"I want to talk to you about Kathleen," I say, then pull

over a chair of my own. She waits until I'm settled, but I can see from the expression on her face that this isn't a conversation that she really wants to have. "How was your lunch with her?"

"Great. She had a wonderful time last night and wanted to thank us for having her over." Her eyes lock onto mine before she rips them away.

"She wasn't uncomfortable at the party? Everyone was friendly to her?"

"She had a great time." Erin shrugs. "It was really good to sit and talk to her for a bit."

"It was really kind of you to invite her and to make sure she'd be dressed well enough to fit in." Erin smiles at me, and I continue, wanting to get to the heart of this faster than we are so I can make sure everything is still on track. "Did Monica or Alexander say something that's making you question your decision?"

She's silent and chews on her lower lip for a moment before giving me a quick nod.

"It's horrible that they got in my head like that," she whispers, and I see the sparkle of tears in the corners of her eyes. "Here I am, wanting nothing more than to help this woman, and Monica said some things last night that actually had me wondering if I'm making the right decision."

"I think you are. Don't you?"

"I do." She sighs and reaches for my hand, linking our fingers together. "I just want to make sure that you and I are on the same page. You really think this is a good idea? You're really going to be behind me one hundred percent, no matter what tests I have to do or what I have to go through to make this happen?"

"One hundred and one percent," I tell her, which makes her smile. "You know me, Erin. You know that I'm not afraid to tell people when I think they're making a mistake about something. I'm not afraid to let them know that they could do something differently, right?"

"I know." Her voice is soft.

"This is no different. Hell, this is even more important to me than anything you or I have ever done before. Believe me, Erin, if I thought there was a chance that I would lose you or something bad would happen to you, I'd never agree to support you on this. I want to keep you safe and healthy, but at the same time, I love your kind heart."

She doesn't say anything, but I can see that I'm getting through to her. "Do you believe me?"

She nods, her eyes wide. "You know I do. Scott, if you weren't behind me and supporting me on this decision, then there's no way I could ever go through with it."

"I do support you. I think you're changing this woman's life. Your life will change too, you know that?"

"Because I don't have two kidneys?" She chuckles, and I know that I won.

Erin won't laugh when she's really upset about something, so when I get her to grin up at me like that, then I know I've finally gotten through to her. "No, because you're going to give someone the gift of life." I lean down to kiss her, brushing my lips across her forehead. "And then you can tell me if you want kids. I'll give you as many as you want, darling."

For a moment, it's silent in the backyard. Erin's barely breathing, like she can't quite believe what I just said. We've talked about this, though.

She thinks I'm finally ready emotionally and financially, but this is much more than that. Once Erin has two healthy kidneys and I don't ever have to worry about her getting sick and not being able to take care of our children, then I'll be ready to have them with her.

Sure, she'll have to recover from the transplant, but she's

in great shape. I can't imagine that it will be difficult for her to bounce right back. The best part is that she'll never be the wiser. She'll live the rest of her life thinking she donated her kidney to Kathleen to save her life.

She'll never know that Dr. Thomas is taking her kidney that might fail and giving her a healthy one from Kathleen's unsuspecting twin. All that matters is that my wife is going to be willing to climb onto that operating table and let the doctor cut her open.

As long as she keeps believing he's there to take her kidney, she'll never question it. There isn't any way she'll ever discover the truth of what happened, and I'll have a perfectly healthy wife.

"After the surgery," she tells me, "we'll make sure that our lives are exactly what we want."

I kiss her again. "After the surgery will be perfect," I agree. "Once you're better than ever." Turning, I walk back into the house and pull my phone from my pocket. Erin is nervous, and we have to make sure that she's entirely on board.

She's nervous. Fix this.

Dr. Thomas doesn't respond.

"**D**id you take care of the problem?" My mom hasn't asked about anything other than Erin from the moment I got back from our picnic yesterday, and it's starting to drive me nuts.

I know I need to answer her because otherwise, she'll just keep asking, but I ignore her, looking down at the phone in my hand like staring at it is going to make it suddenly ring. I've been hoping that Erin would reach out to me today just to check in and let me know that she talked to the doctor, but she hasn't, so I'm going to have to push it along on my own.

Cora comes down the hall, her eyes looking sunken and dark, her skin papery and dry. When I see her in the kitchen door, I slip my phone into my pocket and give her a smile.

"Hey, darling," I tell her. "I thought that you needed more sleep this morning. That's why I didn't get you up for school."

"I don't feel great." She shuffles across the kitchen and settles herself next to my mom at the table before resting her head in her hands. "I was up all night with stomach cramping."

"That's the kidney," I tell her, coming around behind her

to rub her back. "I told you it would get worse, and I guess now you'll listen to me."

She groans and shifts under my touch, so I stop rubbing her and walk over to the refrigerator to get her something to drink. "I wouldn't normally give you soda, but a little ginger ale might help you feel better." Once it's poured, I unscrew a small flask and pour in a little vodka. Not enough to make her drunk, of course, but just enough to keep her feeling terrible. When that's done and the flask is tucked safely back in a drawer, I put the glass in front of Cora and finally turn my attention to my mom.

She's watching me with one eyebrow cocked high like she's not sure of what she's seeing. Ignoring the interested expression on her face, I turn back to my daughter. "Drink up, Cora. I'll let the doctor know you don't feel great, okay?"

She grunts in response and grabs the cold glass, pulling it slowly across the table toward her. I wait until I see her lift her head to take a sip, then pull my phone back out to call Dr. Thomas. He'll want to know she's not feeling good today and that we probably need to get moving on her surgery.

Of course, neither he nor my mom need to know that Cora feels so terrible because of the disulfiram I've been putting in her food. A little bit of that and then some alcohol in her drink is enough to make her feel terrible. Actually making her sick is the only way to ensure that she believes me.

While I'm on the phone with him, I can talk to him about Erin. I'm pretty sure I talked her down from the ledge, but that terrible woman Monica did some damage at the party Saturday night. I know Erin was trying to do something nice for me, but I know Monica and her husband whispered their doubts into her ear the entire time we were all there.

I think I took care of it at the picnic yesterday. I wasn't lying when I told Erin that I really enjoy spending time with her, and it seemed to be just what she needed to hear. At this point, I'll tell her anything I need to as long as she'll willingly show up for the transplant.

I feel like everything is starting to unravel, and I need to juggle a thousand moving pieces to keep things up in the air. Not only do I have to make sure that Erin isn't going to back out when I need her the most, but I also have to keep an eye on Cora.

She's sick, just like I told her she would be. When she argued with me the other day about not feeling bad and how she should be able to go back to school, I knew I would have to do something to get my point across to her. It's hard enough to be trying to take care of your child when she's being pleasant about it, but Cora likes to fight me at every turn.

All it takes is a little something extra in her drink at dinner. Last night, she was particularly rude to me, so I had to bring her down a notch, make her believe me when I tell her she's sick. She'd not wanted to eat what I made, so instead I made her a smoothie using bananas, milk, frozen strawberries, and something special to make her sick. Not so sick that she would die. Not so sick that Dr. Thomas would refuse to do the transplant.

Just sick enough to make sure that she would listen to me when I tell her she needs to take it easy.

My phone buzzes before I have a chance to dial the doctor, and I pick it up, surprised that it's Erin. Hopefully, she has good news for me because I don't think I can handle something else going wrong this morning.

I swallow hard when I think about all the money I've been squirreling away to pay for the double transplant. I'd like to say that Dr. Thomas is giving us a discount, but he's just as money-hungry as the rest of the doctors and lawyers in this town.

It's taken years to get the cash I need for this. Years of ramen for dinner and free lunches for Cora at school. Years of my saving every penny that I make and even cashing in my husband's life insurance policy after he died. I didn't get to use it to pay for a new house like he hoped would happen.

But I'm doing one better. I'm getting both of us kidneys and saving our lives. As soon as the surgery is done, we're out of here. Setting enough aside for passports and plane tickets out of the country made me nervous. What if I don't manage to save enough before the time came that we have the transplants? I have almost enough now, but not quite. What would happen to Cora if I don't get enough put aside?

But it doesn't matter because I'm doing everything I can. I wore the dress that Erin bought me to her party and then took it back to the store yesterday after our picnic. I'd been so careful not to spill on it that I only had one glass of sparkling juice the entire time I was there. Sure, I went home starving, but I was able to return the dress.

And yes, the tag itched me all night long from where it was tucked in under the armhole, but I managed to get the last bit of cash that I need to pay for Dr. Thomas to do the transplants.

If he were going to operate in the hospital, then I'd need to worry about how to pay the hospital bills, but I have a good feeling that they would be mostly written off because we're so poor. But Dr. Thomas wants to perform the surgery in his private office so that nobody is the wiser. If anyone comes looking for money, Cora and I will be gone. Once we get to Russia, where there is no extradition treaty, it won't matter.

Nothing will matter.

Part of me feels a twinge of guilt over what I'm going to do to Erin. I think that we could be friends if the situation were different, but it's not, and we're not, and there's nothing I can do to change the past.

Or the present.

I've been on this path for a long time, and there's no way to get off it now.

All these thoughts run through my head, swirling through it like smoke from a campfire, but then I remember that my phone is still buzzing in my hand, and I need to answer it.

Time is of the essence now. All the pieces are coming together. Erin won't walk away from this, but Cora and I will, and that's all that matters to me.

That's what I tell myself when I pick up the phone and speak to the woman I'm willing to let die so that my daughter and I can live.

My knee keeps bouncing even though I'm doing my best to remain calm. I want to help Kathleen, and it's obvious that Scott thinks this is the right thing for me to do. It's still scary, of course, especially with the actual transplant date growing closer.

No, scratch that. It's not just scary. *It's terrifying.*

What I don't want to admit to myself is just how worried I'm becoming. It was one thing to talk about a transplant in the abstract, but actually going through with it is terrifying. As we get closer and closer to the actual date of the surgery, I feel my nerves acting up. It's hard for me to think about what I'm doing and harder still to bring up my concerns to my husband.

I even called Kathleen this morning just to let her know I was coming in to meet Dr. Thomas. I had a feeling that talking to her would help me feel more confident about my decision, and I was right. She's so thankful, and she's so hopeful that the transplant will happen sooner rather than later that I'm glad I reached out to her on my way here.

Of course, from what I read online, transplants are able to

proceed much faster when it's a private one, like what I'm doing with Kathleen. Unless a person dies and the organ needs to be transplanted immediately, there's always a lot of red tape that has to be worked through before doctors are allowed to operate.

But because Kathleen is so sick and I'm willing to give her a kidney, I guess Dr. Thomas is expediting all of this, which does make me a little bit nervous. I work out and take care of myself, so I know I'm healthy. Nothing should go wrong on my end. Even though we eat a lot of takeout, I make sure it's not super fatty stuff. There's always plenty of quinoa and roasted veggies, fresh fish, and baked chicken. It may sound boring, but I know Scott expects me to look and dress a certain way, and I want to make sure that I keep him happy.

Still, I'm a bundle of nerves that something might be wrong when the nurse finally calls my name. She looks around the waiting room like there's a possibility of someone else being in here too, but I'm the only patient in today. Strange, but I guess that's not unheard of.

Standing up, I follow her down the hall, step obligingly on the scale, then join her in the same small room I sat in to meet Dr. Thomas before. No, I haven't had anything alcoholic to drink since we started this process, yes, I'm sleeping fine, and various other answers to a dozen questions I can't remember, and then she's off, telling me to sit tight and that Dr. Thomas will be in to see me in a moment.

Like I have any other choice.

The walls in here are unlike any other doctor's office I've been in before. Normally, they're covered with posters so you can stare at them while waiting for the doctor to return, but there isn't anything up on the walls in here. It's sterile and cold, the walls a soft beige, and I wish there were a magazine or something for me to read.

Looking at my phone while I wait for him seems rude

because I would hate it if he were to walk in here while I was busy scrolling through social media. I'm pretty quick at getting my phone put away when I want to hide being on it, but I always hate feeling like I'm insulting doctors.

Five minutes tick by. There's a single clock on the wall by the door, and I stare at it, watching the second hand move around the face slowly and surely. It feels surreal, like time has ground to a halt in this office, but it's not like I'm going to get up and walk out.

At the same time, I can't help but wonder exactly what he's doing. There aren't any other patients for him to see right now, that much is obvious, so then where is he?

Just when I'm starting to feel antsy and I'm wondering if I should at least lean out into the hall and look for the nurse— almost half an hour has gone by, to be fair—the door swings open, and Dr. Thomas breezes through, moving quickly like a man on a mission.

I've seen that type of movement a thousand times at home with Scott. When he's in a hurry and feels like he needs to get something done, nothing can stand in his way. It wouldn't matter if he's late for dinner or if there were a super-model in a bikini on the front porch. Scott would blink at her and keep on going to handle whatever he needed to take care of.

I get the feeling that Dr. Thomas is just as focused as my husband, and that's made even more apparent by the fact that the man doesn't even speak to me until he's put his computer down on the counter, sat on the stool, and spun around to look at me.

"There you are," he says, exhaling hard like he just got in from running a marathon. "And thank you for your patience. I was talking with another patient who's a little worked up over her upcoming transplant. You have to stay calm, you know, to make sure that everything will go off without a hitch."

"Of course." I breathe out the words and smile at him. That's why he was late, not because he was doing something fun and ignoring me, but because he was helping another patient. If I were needing some comfort about the upcoming transplant surgery, then I'd definitely want him to spend a little extra time with me.

"I appreciate your understanding," he tells me, inclining his head slightly to me, then turning to pick up his computer. "So I hope you're ready for all the tests we're going to do, but before we get started, I'd like to talk to you."

I lean forward, like I'm actually going to be able to see what he's looking at. There's a flutter of excitement in my chest, just like there always was when I was younger and still in school. Taking tests didn't make me nearly as nervous as I would get when I was waiting for the results.

If I thought that I could get up and look over his shoulder to see exactly what he's looking at, I would do that right now. Unfortunately, before I can even try to decide if moving is a good idea, he closes the computer and puts it back on the counter before fixing his gaze on me.

"You have questions."

I nod, unable to help myself.

"You have doubts."

Shame washes over me, as cool and bracing as if I'd just slipped into a pool in the middle of winter. How this man can tell that just looking at me is beyond me, but I know there isn't any way that I can hide it, so I nod again.

"Of course you do. You're human. If there were a person willing to come in here and donate part of their body to someone else—to a stranger, no less, in your case—and they didn't have doubts? I'd be worried about them, I honestly would."

His kind words make me exhale in relief, but he's not finished.

"Doubts and concerns tell me that you're really thinking this through. That you've talked to other people about it in order to make sure that your mind and heart are in the right place, am I right?" I barely have a chance to nod before he continues like he was already expecting me to agree with him. "Erin, I'm going to be very honest with you. You came here to help Kathleen because you felt determined to do so. You felt like it was the right thing to do, not only for her and her family, but for you. It's easy to let other people spread doubts when you're doing something brave that they wouldn't ever consider doing."

I'm holding my breath. Scott supports me, but I want other people to tell me that I'm doing the right thing, too. Nobody at the party really saw me or got what I'm doing and why I'm doing it. They didn't see how important this was to me and what a big deal it was, not only for me, but for Kathleen. And her family.

Her daughter.

The thought of Kathleen's daughter steels me. I'm not rushing into this. I'm saving a mother. All I want to be is a mom, and hopefully, I'll get the chance to be one when this is all said and done. Giving Kathleen my kidney isn't just saving her, it's making sure that her daughter grows up with her mom.

Kathleen will be able to see her off to prom, watch her graduate college, see her get married. She'll have the opportunity to be there as a grandmother.

"Erin." Dr. Thomas's voice pulls me from the spiral of my thoughts. He's staring right at me, his face so kind that I feel seen for the first time in a while by someone other than my husband. "When someone is willing to go out on a limb to do something extraordinary, then a lot of people can't handle it.

They'll fight you on it, try to pull you back to their own medi-
ocre level. You're better than that."

"I think you're right, but a lot of people told me that they
just want to make sure I'm doing the right thing."

He shakes his head, brushing away my concerns as easily
as if they were smoke from an extinguished candle. "You're
extraordinary, Erin. Very few people would be willing to do
what you're doing for a complete stranger. Don't listen to the
world around you telling you that it's wrong. They're saying
that because they don't understand it, not because it's true."

That's it. I latch onto his words like they're a life vest and
I'm out at sea in a terrible storm. Dr. Thomas understands
that I'm doing this not for me, not to show off to other people,
but because I'm called to help in a way other people simply
aren't willing to.

"You're one of the special ones," Dr. Thomas tells me. His
voice is lower now, like he's afraid that someone is going to
overhear. I lean forward, wanting to soak up every single
word that he's saying. "To give so selflessly so that someone
else may live? It's amazing."

"I only wish I could save more than one person," I say.
The words just flow out of me like a river. I don't even think
about them. They're just there, so honest and raw that I
expect him to frown or flinch away from them, but a smile
widens on his face, and I feel like I just said the perfect thing.

For the first time, I'm fitting in. No, it's not that. I'm
standing out, but in the best way possible. I realize all of a
sudden that I want to please this kind doctor with the deep
brown eyes. I don't care that he was late to our appointment. I
like the way he's talking to me and treating me like he is so
proud of who I am.

It's the same support that I'm getting from home, but it
feels different coming from the doctor. There's no way that

he'd go through with this surgery if he thought something bad would happen to me, right?

That's what I keep telling myself. I have to trust him, even though there's a small voice in the back of my head that's worried I'm making a mistake.

"I understand what you mean," he tells me, never taking his eyes away from my gaze. "And I think you might be able to. Just stay open to how you can help, Erin, and I believe you will change lives."

I'll change lives. Those three words are some of the kindest ones I've ever heard, and I know in this moment that I don't care what Alexander or Monica or anyone else has to say.

Kathleen needs me. I'll do anything for her.

Because that's the kind of person I am.

26

KATHLEEN

The carpet in our home is terribly thin, and I'm wearing a path in it walking from the kitchen to the bedroom and then back again while I wait for the phone to ring. I should be embarrassed about the state of the house, but it's not like we're going to live here for much longer. Once the surgery is complete and Cora and I can travel, then we'll be gone.

Then it won't matter what the crappy carpet looks like. It won't matter that the front yard is mostly dirt and rocks and that nothing seems to want to grow there. All that will matter is that I have a good kidney and that I'll have done everything I can to keep Cora from having to be on the transplant list.

Even as I think that, I know that giving her a kidney isn't a total guarantee. I got my first kidney years ago, back when I was a lot younger. I took every precaution, and I honestly thought everything was going to be okay. I didn't think there would be an issue with the kidney.

Sure, I read the pamphlets. I knew about the risk of chronic rejection, which can happen so slowly over the course of a few years as your body fights the kidney that you might not even know it's happening. All of that information is given to you before you sign any papers, before you go anywhere near the waiting list, but I still didn't believe it would ever happen.

Nobody thinks that something terrible is going to happen to them. The odds were in my favor, or that's what my doctor had told me time and time again. Even with the odds in my favor, though, something terrible happened, and my body decided to fight. Not *for* me, not to save my life, but to reject the kidney that was supposed to save me.

I remember getting the tests back from my doctor. I'd gone in for an appointment so worried that I wasn't feeling good, worried that it was all happening again. Of course, there was a chance that it was all in my head. That happens from time to time with people. People think that they're sick, and they end up at the doctor's office all the time.

But that's not what happened with me. It took a few tests to figure it out, but when I learned the truth, that my body was fighting against the kidney and trying to reject it, it honestly felt like I already knew it. It was a truth that I was convinced of, and my doctor was finally just telling me what I already knew.

That was when I knew I wasn't just going to fight for me, but also for my baby girl. I knew right then that I had to save her from this same fate. If I could get her a kidney that was the perfect match now, before hers turned bad in her body, then I wouldn't feel so bad about the fact that I wouldn't ever be able to give her one of mine.

As her mother, my job is to protect her. To save her. I hate that I'm never going to be able to do that with my own kidney, but that's why I swore I would do everything I could to get her one of her own.

My mom had been taking care of me as I got sicker and needed my first transplant. After the transplant, I moved out of my mom's house and took Cora away, but when I got sick again, I came back. It was hard to move across the country and back in with my mom, but then I found Dr. Thomas. He was the only doctor who seemed to really care, not only about me, but also about Cora. We began tests for her at the same time that Dr. Thomas started tests on me again to see how long I had with my failing kidney.

Not long.

Of course, he hadn't been too keen on performing a transplant on her without her being terribly sick, but that was easy to take care of. I know firsthand what a failing kidney feels like, what it looks like, and even though the tests came back inconclusive, it would be impossible for anyone to look at my baby girl and think she wasn't sick.

That was all on me.

It's almost killed me knowing that I'm the one making her sick all the time, but someone had to be willing to do it. Someone had to be willing to stand up and do what needed to be done so that I can keep her safe in the future, and I'm her mom. It had to be me.

My phone suddenly vibrates in my pocket, and I wipe my palm on my jeans before pulling it out. Cora and my mom are in the living room, watching some trash TV, and I duck out the back door onto the little wooden stoop to take the call.

"Dr. Thomas?" I cringe when I hear the hope in my voice. He has to know that he has this effect on people, but this entire time, I've tried to remain as calm as possible.

"Kathleen, are you sitting down?"

"Yes," I lie. From here, I can see straight into the neighbor's backyard. There was a fence between the two properties years ago, but it fell down after a huge wind storm last summer, and neither of us had the ambition to repair it. I don't have the energy or the cash, not with everything I have going toward Dr. Thomas's fees when this is all said and done, and the neighbor usually sits out back drinking, so it's pretty obvious that fixing the fence isn't high on his to-do list either.

"Good. I wanted to let you know that I just spoke to Erin and she's all in. That little party over the weekend almost changed her mind, but she's back on track now."

I exhale hard with relief and now do sag down to the stoop. I don't want to sit down on the dirty wood, but I feel like my legs are suddenly unable to hold me up. "What now? How much longer do we have to wait until we can do this?"

Without thinking, I reach down and lightly trace my scar through my shirt. Seeing it there every single day, marring my skin, reminding me of the fact that I had a second chance at life and it slipped through my fingers makes me angry. I want the new scar, want a second chance.

For me and for Cora.

"When we met today and talked, I got the feeling that she's a bit nervous. The last thing we want is for her to change her mind, although I think you're doing a good job of keeping her on track. I'm getting all the pieces in order, don't you worry."

There's something I want to ask him, but I know there isn't any kind way to do it. Biting my lower lip, I watch as the neighbor comes out onto his back porch, a beer in his hand. He sits down in an old lawn chair and sighs before popping the tab. It's so still out while I wait to respond to Dr. Thomas that I hear the noise in the quiet.

"Kathleen? Are you still there?"

I clear my throat. "I know this is going to sound insensitive," I say, keeping my voice as low as possible so my neighbor doesn't hear me. By the looks of him, though, this isn't his first beer of the day, and I doubt that he's going to pay any attention to what I'm saying. "But how quickly can we get this done? If she's nervous, shouldn't we hurry it up?"

A slight pause, and I wonder for a moment if I said something I shouldn't have. We've been so careful not to talk about our real plan over the phone just in case someone were to overhear us, but I don't feel like driving to his office just to approach him with this one question.

"That's something to consider," he says, his voice suddenly crisp and clear. In my mind, I can picture a nurse leaning into his office to ask him something. "But the surgery itself is going to be long and complicated, given its nature, and I need to make sure that we take every precaution possible to ensure that it goes as smoothly as possible."

In other words, no, I'm not pushing this surgery up.

I hear him talking to someone else, and I wait, digging my nails into the rotting boards I'm sitting on. This house was a definite downgrade from where we used to live, but when I knew I had to start saving for this big surgery, I was willing to sell our larger house and move here.

Everyone assumed that it was because of unpaid hospital bills. They're not wrong, exactly. Only this time, I'm not writing a single check to the hospital. It's all going directly to Dr. Thomas.

"Listen, Kathleen," he suddenly says, his voice so low that I press the phone hard into my ear to hear him. "If you don't want to go through the pain of finding a kidney again, then I need to make sure that she's not going to back out. Do you understand that?"

"I do," I whisper, but he's already hung up. He's angry, that much is obvious by the way he hissed the words at me and the dull sound of the ringtone in my ear.

The man who is going to save my life is mad at me. I shiver, wrapping my arms around my legs and pulling them up to my chest while I watch my neighbor. All that matters is that Erin isn't backing out.

Not yet, anyway.

But she won't. I just have to see to that.

27

SCOTT

Time marches steadily on, and I know I need to get home to Erin and see what she has planned for dinner, but there are just a few things I want to do before I leave the office. Normally, I don't care if Erin goes into my home office to check on me when I'm working or even if she has to close the browser after I've been online.

I'm not the type of man who has anything to hide. Erin doesn't have anything to hide from me, either, or I'd know about it.

She's always honest with me, and I'm as honest with her as possible. I just don't see having trackers and cameras as keeping a secret from her. Everything I do is to keep my wife healthy and safe. She's worth it all.

But I reached out to Dr. Thomas today to make sure everything is still on track, and haven't heard back yet. There's no way Erin would ever forgive me for lying to her about this donation or orchestrating it in the first place, which is why she simply can't ever find out that I was behind it all. If she did . . . well, let's just say I have a pretty good feeling that Erin would be more upset about that than I am about the chicken piccata from the bistro down the street.

That's why I don't want to be looking into the good doctor or Kathleen when I'm at home. It's best to keep Erin as far away from the truth as possible.

Kathleen has a twin who thinks she's giving her kidney to her sister. Thankfully, due to the money I'm paying him, that healthy kidney will be coming to Erin. He's shown me test results to prove to me that the twin is healthy.

Part of me feels bad for the twin and for Kathleen, but it's not my fault that they don't have someone like me looking out for them. I'll do anything for Erin, and I'm not letting any concern I have for Kathleen get in the way of my wife's health.

I type in Kathleen's name before I realize that I don't know her last name, so there's no way to search for her. This entire time, I've been trusting Dr. Thomas blindly, but I'm done doing that now. He won't give me information, but maybe I can find out more about Kathleen on my own. Instead of giving up, though, I continue my search, adding *kidney transplant* and our town after her name and crossing my fingers that I'll find something.

I didn't think I'd find her social media, so I'm not disappointed by that, but buried on the bottom of the first page of search results is a link to an article that interests me.

Kidney Recipients Get New Lease on Life

It's from just over a decade ago, talking about her needing a kidney. I frown and double-check the date before clicking on the link. Sure, it's entirely possible that the website has the date wrong on the article, but that doesn't seem terribly likely. It's weird, but I'm sure there's a logical explanation.

The page loads quickly, but before I can start reading,

Alexander pops his head into my office. "You busy?" He has a look on his face that tells me that even if I am busy, I'd better figure out how to become unbusy as quickly as possible.

I minimize the window and give him a shrug. "Just checking my email. What's up?"

"Good. Listen. About the case tomorrow. We just got some new evidence, and the DA is going to be ticked when they find out that it wasn't included in discovery."

"That's not good." Alexander is still standing in my office door, so I turn off my computer before pushing back from my desk to join him. "What kind of evidence is it? Do you really think we need it for the case, or is it something we don't need to have in order to win?"

He blows a raspberry and rolls his eyes. "Listen, I don't know how best to tell you this, but this is the type of evidence that can keep our man from doing years in jail. A neighbor across the street from the house where the murders were committed has a security system and just now admitted all of that and brought in the tape."

"Why now?" We're walking quickly down the hall, eating up the distance between our offices and a room where we have a huge TV set up for viewing evidence. "They finally realize that holding back evidence like that is a big no-no?"

"Apparently, he's terrible with technology. He's a few cards short of a full deck, so I have no idea what suddenly inspired him to pull the footage or even how he managed to get his hands on equipment like this. It's not cheap."

"An alcoholic in that neighborhood with a security camera? I hate to say it, but it's probably stolen."

"It's probably stolen," he says at the same time as I do. "Jinx, you owe me a beer. And trust me, once we get out of here tonight and finally have our minds wrapped around what the hell we're going to do, you're going to need one."

I know there's not going to be an easy way for me to get

out of this little meeting with Alexander, so I pull my phone from my pocket and fire off a quick text to Erin, letting her know that I'm going to be terribly late. There's even a room down the hall with cots set up for lawyers to sleep in when they're spending too much time on a case to go home, but so far, I've managed to avoid spending the night there.

I'd much rather be at home in my own bed, snuggled next to my wife, and eating breakfast in my own kitchen the next morning. It's one thing to work late here, but another entirely to have to spend the night on the cots.

She'll be disappointed, but I'm even more so. Sighing, I sit down in one of the chairs that face the TV and wait for Alexander to turn it on. It's obvious that he's been watching the footage already. There's a still on the screen, and I lean back, stretching out my back.

The reason we're the best law firm in the area is because we're devoted. I love my job and give everything I have to it, but Alexander goes above and beyond. As much as I hate to admit it to myself, we're going to be here for hours.

All the research that I wanted to do on Kathleen suddenly seems way less important than it was five minutes ago. If I hadn't sat down to dig into the woman my wife wants to give a kidney to, then I'd already be on my way home.

And called back just as quickly.

No, there's no way out of this. We're in the courtroom tomorrow, and the time for discovery has passed, but if this evidence is really as good as Alexander is saying it is, then we're going to have to figure out what we're going to do about it.

That means I have to push all thoughts of Kathleen and my wife from my mind. After all, it's not like the surgery is coming up anytime soon. There's nothing for me to do about it right now.

Erin's fully on board. She knows that this is a matter of life or death, after all.

"Late again," I mutter, tapping hard at my screen and then setting the phone down with a *thunk* on the counter. Turning back to the stove, I eyeball the food I have bubbling away and sigh. It's not like I made it all myself, so it's not like I spent hours on my feet working over a hot stove, but it still drives me nuts that I have this delicious meal and Scott won't be home to share it with me.

I know Alexander. If there's even the hint of their having to work late, then I'm sure that Ritzy's, the local pizza joint, is already delivering a few pies and sodas there for them to make it through their work. Not only will they snack on it all evening, but it'll be there waiting for them in the morning when they get in and want a greasy breakfast.

"Gross," I say, turning off the stove and glaring once more at the food. It's not the chicken's fault, but the longer it's on the heat, the more likely it is that it's going to get tough.

I'm about to pack everything up into glass storage containers and put it in the fridge when my phone vibrates. Hope springs up in me that it might be Scott, and I grab my phone quickly, suddenly a little disappointed that it wasn't Scott who texted until I see Kathleen's name on the screen.

You free for dinner?

That's weird. It's almost like she was watching me and knew right when Scott told me that he wasn't going to make it home for dinner. I know I'm just being paranoid, but I still walk to the kitchen window and lift the curtain to peek outside.

Nothing. Of course. What did I expect, that she would be standing on my front porch, a Tupperware of ambrosia salad in her hand, waving at me and waiting for me to let her in?

It's not that she's watching me, it's just that we're so connected. I felt the connection the first time I met her.

Actually, I am! You hungry? Come on over?

I send the text before really stopping to think about it, but I'm sure Scott won't be mad. Right now, he's probably face-first in a huge slice of supreme pizza, and he definitely won't want reheated chicken tomorrow. I'll have to order something else, but that won't be a problem. When you're on a first-name basis with everywhere in town, then the chefs make sure that your order is made perfectly for you.

Besides, I like Kathleen, and I don't particularly want to be alone tonight when Scott's going to be late. Sometimes, I fire up a movie and eat dinner on the sofa when he's late, but it can get lonely. At least with a friend coming over, I won't have to be all alone.

Be there in ten!

Great. I have no idea where Kathleen lives, and it hits me that I've never asked her. I should find out more about her, not only because she's the person I'm going to be saving, but also because I want her to stay in my life when this is all said and done. I know she's not my daughter, and it's silly to even think of her in that way, but I can't help but feel like we have an amazing connection that I don't want to lose after the transplant.

All I really know about Kathleen is that she was dealt a terrible hand in life, she has a daughter, and she seems to really like me.

It sounds crazy to admit, but I *like* being liked. I'm glad she wants to spend time with me and that she seems to really enjoy my company. Once the transplant is complete and we're both healthy, I can only imagine how much fun it will be to have her in my life.

I bet she'd love to do some traveling with me. There's no guarantee that I'll be able to get pregnant right away, and we can travel together until I have kids.

Turning from the window, I turn the stove back on and set the table, swapping out the wineglass I had for Scott for another water glass and filling it with ice water. A few slices of lemon in our glasses make them look really fancy, and I'm just lighting a candle when the doorbell rings.

"Hi," I say, swinging the door open for her. Kathleen has a matching smile on her face and grins at me before wiping her shoes on the doormat and stepping inside. "I'm really glad you texted. Scott had just told me that he wasn't going to make it home for dinner."

"Oh, really? Perfect timing. Seriously, thanks for letting me come over. It was feeling a little claustrophobic in my house tonight, and I needed a bit of a break." She steps to the side as I shut the front door, and then follows me into the kitchen. "This smells amazing! I don't know how you do it all

—the cooking and cleaning—and still look like a million bucks."

I laugh, smoothing down the front of my apron. "I'm lucky because I've never had to work outside the house," I tell her with a shrug. "I always told Scott that I'd be happy to get a job, but he never wanted me to work outside the house, so I haven't."

She grins and leans against the counter, looking more at home now than she did when she was here for the big dinner party. Then she was dressed to the nines in clothes that I'm sure would make anyone jealous, but today she has on jeans with a hole in one knee, a sweater that has definitely seen better days, and has her hair pulled back in a low pony with some strands already escaping.

She looks more suited to work in the garden than to eat dinner from my china, but I push that thought away. We can't all be as fortunate as I am, and it's up to me to share some of that with others. Sure, I could easily act like a dragon and hoard all of my money and my kidneys, but I'm not going to be that person.

I plate the food quickly and then turn to look at her. "Hey, I saw Dr. Thomas today," I tell Kathleen, who looks pleased.

"I remember your saying that! How did it go?" She takes two plates of food from me and carries them to the table while I turn off the stove. When I join her, I rest my elbows on the table and look at her through the steam rising from the food before answering.

"Great. I have to admit to you that I was a little nervous going into that appointment."

"That's normal, I think. I'm pretty nervous too, and I'm not the one giving up an organ." She laughs and takes a sip of water. "But you're back on track?"

I know what she's asking. She wants to know if my head is still in the game or if I'm going to back out of the donation.

She's curious whether I've been stringing her along all this time or if I'm going to save her life.

When I really look at her, I notice some tightness around her eyes. She's stressed, and for good reason. How many people did she say she'd had offer to give her a kidney, yet they all backed out on her? I don't remember the exact number, but I can only imagine how that would wear on you.

No wonder she was so concerned when we first met. No wonder that, even after all of my reassurances, she still looks nervous. It's one thing to let someone borrow your car, but this is on an entirely different level.

And Dr. Thomas had told me that was what made me so special. I'm not going to back out like so many other people have. I saw a need and knew that I could fill it, and I'm going to.

"I was a little bit scared," I admit, looking her in the eyes. I want to ask her how young she is, because it's obvious that I'm older than her. Being around her makes me feel like I could be her big sister.

Or her mom.

That makes me smile.

"In fact, I was more than scared. At the party, there were some comments made that had me questioning whether I was doing the right thing or if I was going to regret it, so I'm really glad I met with Dr. Thomas today."

She hasn't lifted her fork. She's staring at me like she's waiting for the other shoe to drop, like she knows that something terrible is about to come out of my mouth and her entire world is going to fall apart.

"But he helped me see the light," I say, and her shoulders visibly relax a little. "He reminded me of why I'm doing this, which is to help you. It's not about me; it's not about the people who might have something to say. I want to help, and that scares some people."

"It does." She nods, then reaches across the table to me and squeezes my hand hard. "It scares people to do what's right, Erin, and you have to remind yourself that you're bigger than that. That you're braver and stronger, and you're not going to let a little bit of fear stand between you and the right thing."

"Exactly." I suck in a shaky breath. This woman gets me more than a lot of other people. She sees into me and sees my heart, just like Dr. Thomas does. "You know, it's silly, because we barely just met, but I feel connected to you. I hope we can stay in each other's lives after all of this. Be friends. Do brunch. I think that this could be the start of a beautiful friendship."

She responds by letting go of my hand and lifting her water glass to me in cheers. "To friends," she says, and I touch my glass to hers, my eyes locked on her face. "I will always carry a part of you with me, and I won't ever forget you, no matter how much time passes."

29

She's too easy.

I shouldn't delight so much in being able to control Erin, but I do. It's nice to know that I can convince her that I'm some pathetic charity case she should help when really, I'm in complete control of the situation.

Sure, there is part of me that almost feels bad because I like her, but you can't have everything in life, and I'd rather have my health and my daughter than a friend.

Coming home from dinner with Erin, I kick my shoes off on the front porch and let myself in with my key. It's not late by any means, but I'm surprised when I see that Cora isn't in the living room with my mom.

"Where's Cora?" I ask, locking the front door, even though it's not like anyone would try to break in here. We don't have anything worth taking, and if they did want to get in, the lock is just a false sense of security. I'm pretty sure that you can just jiggle the door hard in its frame and the entire thing will swing right open.

"She said she wasn't feeling good, so she went to bed." My

mom pins me in place with a hard stare. "Said that her stomach was upset and she was feeling bloated."

"That's the kidney failure," I say, going to sit on the sofa next to her. She shifts away from me a little bit so that she can look at me, but I don't turn to meet her gaze. "I'm not surprised that it's happening, Mom. You remember how sick I started getting when I was younger. It's like you wake up one day and your body is falling apart." I snap my fingers in the air to make my point.

"Something like that." She touches me on the shoulder to get my attention. I don't want to turn to look at her, but I finally do. "What are you doing, Kathleen?" Her voice is a low whisper, and I shiver, doing my best to hold her gaze with mine.

"What am I doing?" My voice is just as low. "I'm saving her life."

She shakes her head. "Are you? Or are you just tormenting the poor thing? I know that you're making her sick. Stop this madness. Get the kidney you need to live and then let Cora have her own life. It's one thing if she were actually sick, but you're doing this to her."

I can't believe what my mother is saying to me. For a moment I just stare at her, trying to tell whether she's being serious or not. She's unblinking, her eyes locked on mine like that will change my mind about what I have to do.

You know what? I don't have to listen to this. Out of all of the people in the world, my mom should know what it's like to watch your child be sick and know the sinking feeling that you can't do anything about it. She watched my kidney fail, and she's getting to watch it happen again. I haven't told her what I'm doing with Cora, but she's more observant than I imagined. Still, I'm not going to stop.

I can't stop.

"I have to save her," I hiss, digging my nails into my thighs to keep my focus. I want to scream at her, but that would bring Cora out of her room to see what's going on, and I can't have that. "You have no idea what it's like to know that your body is failing."

"But hers isn't," she insists, giving my shoulder a little shake. "Not yet, anyway, but it's going to fail if you keep giving her things to make her sick."

I stare at her. "I thought you were on board with the plan. I thought you agreed with it!"

"When you told me that she was really sick, of course I was! I want what's best for both of you. But if you're the one making her sick and she doesn't really need a transplant, then what are you doing?"

"You don't love her like I do," I tell my mom. My voice is cold, and I wonder if she's going to flinch away at the sharp edges of my words, but she doesn't. "You're just not willing to do what it takes to save her."

"I'm not interested in seeing her go through unnecessary surgery! She doesn't have to face this, Kathleen, not yet, not until there isn't any choice. Why are you pushing it so hard? She's your little girl! How can you do this to her?"

Now I spring to my feet, letting her hand fall from my shoulder. "I'm pushing it because I'm here to push it," I say, leaning down to speak to her. "I'm pushing it now because I won't be here to do it in the future, and I want to do everything I can to save my daughter. If you were half the mother I am, then you would understand that."

"Kathleen!" My mom stands up too, a little shaky on her feet. Maybe if she didn't stay on the sofa all day long, watching TV and eating junk food, then she wouldn't be so wobbly right now, but I don't care. All I care about is saving Cora.

"Push it," I dare her. "Push it and see what will happen. I'll destroy anyone who tries to stand between me and what I need to do for Cora. I don't care who it is or what they're trying to do, I will destroy them. That means you, Mom."

She's breathing shallowly, and I watch as her hand flutters up to her chest. "It hurts," she whispers, but I shake my head. Sure, her heart has always been bad, but I'm not interested in her trying to guilt me into feeling bad over what I'm doing for me and for Cora.

"You're doing it to yourself. Stop trying to keep me from saving my little girl." Spinning away from her, I stalk down the hall to the bathroom. There's only one in this house, just one bathroom for the three of us to share. When Cora and I move and start our new lives, I want to live somewhere where we have at least three bathrooms so we always have one more than we need.

It'll feel decadent, not stepping all over each other each time we have to take a piss.

There's a small medicine cup on the counter, and I grab it, hurriedly filling it to the top with a mixture of vodka and cranberry juice that I keep under the sink. She's had the disulfiram recently enough that all I need to do is get a little alcohol in her system to keep her feeling terrible. Once I have a small cup of it, I hurry down the hall to Cora's room. A caring mother would want to check in on her child and make sure that they felt okay, and that's just what I'm going to do.

Pushing open the door, I rap it twice with my knuckles to let Cora know I'm coming in. Her desk lamp is on, casting a soft glow throughout the room. She's on her bed, turned away from me, covers pulled up over her, but I don't think she's asleep.

"Darling?" I ask, sitting down on the edge of her bed and rubbing her back. "What's going on?"

"I feel terrible." Her voice breaks with tears, and regret washes over me, but it's only there for a moment.

I'm doing what I have to do. I'm doing what any good mother would do if they really loved their child and wanted to take care of them.

"That's what Grandma said," I say, pulling her toward me so that she rolls onto her back. "I brought you some medicine."

"I don't want it." She tries to curl back up into a little ball.

But I stop her, pushing down harder on her shoulder to make her turn to me. "I don't always want my medicine either, Cora, but when the doctor says it's what you have to have, then we're going to do it, okay? This is just a little something to help take away the stomach pain and make you feel better in the morning."

She sighs and pushes herself up to a sit, letting me wrap my arm around her to support her. She's so thin, and I'm actually surprised when I get a good look at her face.

Cora's skin is papery and thin, and she doesn't have very much color in her cheeks. Her eyes look sunken into her face, and her lips are dry. "Take this," I tell her, holding out the little cup and waiting for her to take it. Her fingers tremble a little bit when she takes it from me, but she tips it dutifully up to her lips and swallows it down.

"Good girl," I whisper, putting the cup and medicine down on her bedside table. There's some Chapstick there, and I grab the tube, running it over her lips for her to try to combat how terribly dry they are. "That will help, okay? Do you want anything to eat?"

"No." She moans a little as she lies back down. For a moment, I sit on the edge of her bed, unsure of what to do, but then I kick off my shoes and turn, pulling the covers up over me as well and looping my arm around my daughter to pull her close.

She doesn't resist. Instead, she snuggles back into me, and I kiss the back of her head.

"It's going to be okay, Cora. I promise you, once we get the transplant for you, then you're going to feel so much better. You'll have energy to run and play with your friends, and you'll be able to concentrate without your head feeling fuzzy. Trust me, this is the right thing for you."

She doesn't respond, but I don't need her to. I'm doing the right thing, no matter what my mom might try to say to me. She doesn't know what it's like to love someone as much as I love Cora.

I know that she'll come through it on the other side better and stronger, and one day, she'll look back on everything and will thank me.

She'll know that I'm the reason she feels so good. She'll know that she never had to wait on the transplant list for an organ that might never come.

A twinge of guilt eats at me when I think about the fact that Erin is going to have to die so that Cora and I can both live. She was so kind at dinner, making sure I had enough to eat, laughing at my jokes.

When she told me that she thought that the two of us should be friends when this is all said and done, I wasn't sure what to say to her. It's not like we're going to be able to hang out after the surgery, but I have to keep her on board. Telling her that I want to be friends with her was a smart way to make sure she didn't back out on me. It's one thing to say that you want to help someone, and another entirely to actually do it. The closer we get to the transplant, the more afraid I am that she'll get cold feet. She's the kindest person I know and the only one I can imagine being willing to give up so much so that my daughter and I can have the best lives possible.

But she's right. If she wasn't going to die, then I think that maybe we could be friends. I'd like to have brunch with her and let her take me shopping. *No, that can't happen.* I shake my head. We're from two different worlds and would never be able to be friends, but I wasn't joking when I said that I'd always carry a part of her with me. So will Cora, but Erin can't know that.

30

The next morning, I finally uncurl myself from around Cora, check her breathing to make sure that it's nice and even, then wander down the hall to pee and brush my teeth. I'm still in the same clothes from when I went to dinner with Erin, and they feel stiff and uncomfortable, but I'll check in on my mom before taking a shower.

She's already up. I can hear the TV down the hall from the bathroom, even with the door closed, and I roll my eyes as I rinse out my mouth and head into the living room to say hi to her.

Part of me wants to see how she slept, but there's another part of me that just wants to make sure that she calmed down from last night. The last thing I need is for her to be working against me while I'm trying to save Cora's life.

"You know that you're going to rot your brain watching TV all the time," I say, striding into the room. She doesn't respond, and I glance at her once before doing a double take. "Mom?"

Instead of sitting ramrod straight in the corner like usual, she's slumped over to the side of the sofa, her mouth slightly open, her eyes staring off into the corner of the room.

"Mom?" I take a staggering step into the room, my heart beating in my chest like a wild creature. "Mom!"

She doesn't move.

The air suddenly feels closed up and tight, and I suck in a breath, trying to clear my head. It's like the walls of the room are shifting in on me. The room seems to tilt, and it feels like the floor suddenly shifts under my feet. I reach out, feeling for the walls of the room, but my fingers brush against air, and I suck in a breath as I stumble forward.

"Mom!" My voice is ripped from my throat, and I fall down on my knees in front of the sofa, clutching at her hands. There's no warmth in them, no soft touch that I've grown so accustomed to. Still, I link our fingers together and squeeze them hard, trying to get her to look at me.

Did I kill my mother?

The thought is terrifying, and I drop her hand, my skin crawling at the cool sensation of hers. I reach up to grab my throat, letting out a strangled cry. Our last conversation had been an argument, but I didn't think that her heart was so bad that it would push her over the edge. Guilt wraps around me, and I feel like I can't breathe.

"Mom, is everything okay?" Cora's voice trembles, and I whip around to look at her. My eyes are wide, and I feel like I still can't catch my breath, but when I see my daughter standing there in the door, I know I need to pull myself together.

"Cora," I say, pushing myself up to stand. My legs feel like Jell-O, like I just ran a marathon, and I have to focus hard to keep them from giving out from under me. "Cora, don't look."

"Is she dead?" Instead of sounding terrified, she sounds interested, and I'm shocked when she walks right up to me. I turn to her, grabbing at her arm to keep her from going any farther, but she pushes my hands out of the way. "Let me see her."

"Cora, don't look," I tell her, but she's already kneeling down in front of my mom. I watch with surprise as she gently takes my mom's hands in hers and rubs them like that's going to wake her up or bring some feeling back into her skin. "I'm going to call the police," I stammer, turning away from the scene.

It's too much for me to watch my daughter touch my dead mother like that. I should stay with her, should keep an eye on the two of them, but I turn away, my fingers fumbling as I stab at the phone.

The dispatcher is friendly. Her voice is light and airy, like she's on vacation on the beach, and I somehow manage to fumble out the words. "My mom died," I say, then give her my address. She parrots it back to me and tells me to stay on the line, but I hang up, unable to listen to her breathing in my ear.

"They're coming," I tell Cora, pulling her up to me so that I can hug her. "They'll be here as soon as possible, okay? Let's go outside, get some fresh air."

"I don't want fresh air." Her voice is stronger than I thought it would be, but there are tears streaming down her face. "I want to be with her!"

I should stay. I should be here with her to make sure she's mentally okay, but right now, I need to get out of the house. Turning away from my daughter, I rush outside to wait for the officers. They'll be here in a bit, but I have a feeling that there won't be any hurry for them to get to our house.

It's not like our address is in the nicest neighborhood in town, and I just told them that my mother was already dead. Even if they were to show up in just five minutes, there wouldn't be anything they would be able to do for her.

I wish I had a glass of wine or a cigarette to take off the

edge, but I don't, and I can't have either of those. Even if I weren't facing down another transplant, having something like that would only make me feel worse in the long run.

Leaning against the rail, I try to calm my breaths. Slow sips of air in my nose and out through my mouth make me feel a little bit better, but I'm still feeling slightly out of control. This wasn't supposed to happen. My mother and I don't—didn't—always get along, but that doesn't mean I want her dead. It doesn't mean I don't want her around.

Of course, we'd be saying goodbye eventually anyway, when Cora and I left the country. I know that the two of us aren't going to be able to stay here, not once the transplants are complete and people realize that Erin is missing.

My heart aches when I realize that I want to reach out to her and tell her that my mom just died. I want to hear what comforting words she might be able to share with me, because I have a feeling that she'd have some. I don't have anyone else. Part of the plan has involved my making sure that Cora and I don't get too close to people.

Anyone who would become suspicious of what I'm doing or the plan to leave the country with her had to be cut out of our lives, no matter how hard that's been. It's all been almost impossible for my daughter, every last bit of it. Sure, she has other students at school she likes to talk to, but I haven't let her have them over to hang out. I can't. We have to keep that separation so it's easy for us to leave.

But that means I don't have anyone right now. I want a friend whom I can turn to and talk about how terrible this is, but there isn't anyone I can rely on. Erin's the only person I know I could call right now for help, but it's stupid to even consider getting closer to her.

Can you imagine? Getting even closer to the woman I'm going to kill so that my daughter and I can live?

Panic grips the back of my neck, and I suck in another

breath, trying to tell myself that everything is going to be okay. All I can do right now is wait for the ambulance to come. They'll make sure that my mom is really dead, even though I know there isn't a chance that she's actually still alive; then they'll take her body away.

After that, Cora and I simply carry on as planned. We have the transplants with Dr. Thomas. He gets rich off the work he does on the two of us, and we get new lives. Erin gets nothing.

My mind is silent as I grip the deck railing and wait for the police.

A little while later, the police and EMTs arrive. Streaming through the house like ants, I can just imagine what they're thinking about our tiny little home. It's not nice, not by any means, but there's no way I can tell them that the reason it's so run-down and small is because we're saving every last penny we have to pay for two transplants.

I feel their eyes drift across my face and land on Cora's, and I stiffen when one EMT leans over to whisper to another. She looks terrible this morning. What I gave her last night was designed to make her feel terrible, not to improve her health. But hopefully, to them, she looks like just a sick kid, one whose grandmother just died in the living room.

"It was an unattended death," one of the officers says to me. He has kind eyes, but I've noticed that he's done everything in his power since getting here to keep from touching anything. None of them want to be in here, and I can just imagine them all going back to the station and talking about how dirty my house is.

He hasn't said anything of the sort to me, but I still feel myself bristle.

"I was here with her," I counter. "It wasn't unattended. And she's had heart problems forever, so it's not totally unexpected." *I killed my mother.* Swallowing hard, I stare at him, pushing that thought from my mind.

"You said you found her like this. Even in cases like this, when death wasn't a total surprise, because she wasn't sick and in the hospital or on hospice, we like to have an ME take a peek and make sure that everything is okay." He leans forward a little bit like the two of us are sharing some big secret and drops his voice when he speaks again. "Doing so will allow us to transfer the body to the hospital for you. Unless you'd rather find another way yourself."

Oh. I shake my head. "Thank you," I whisper. Behind him, I see two EMTs loading my mom onto a stretcher. Cora's off to the side, her eyes locked on the scene. I should go to her. I should try to comfort my daughter over what she just saw and how terrible it is to lose my mom, but I don't feel like I can move.

Instead, I stand apart from her, watching the officers and EMTs stream out of the house with my mom in tow.

No, not my mom. He called her the body.

Still, my fingers itch to call Erin. I need to reach out to her and have someone comfort me, but how can I do that when she's going to be just a body soon, too?

My eyes flick to Cora, and I feel my resolve stiffen. I have to be strong for her. As much as I'd love a friend, I want my daughter more, especially now that I just lost my mom. I need a kidney to survive, and she needs one to feel better, so Erin can't be my friend, no matter how much I want her to.

She's an organ donor. Nothing more.

31

ERIN

I 'm feeling antsy, but I can't put my finger on why. Time seems to be flying by, but I'm still ready for the transplant to get here faster. I just want it over with. Scott has been amazing this whole time, of course. He's always supportive, always letting me do what I think is right while still making sure that he's there to take care of me.

So time has been passing quickly, and all I can do recently is think about the upcoming transplant. It's always on my mind, no matter what I'm doing.

My plan for the day is to clean the house, which is something I really hate doing. I have a cleaning crew to do that for me, although I do try to tidy right at the last possible minute before Scott gets home. Now that the time is here for me to actually get started dusting, though, I don't want to. Instead, I stand in the middle of the living room, turning in a circle, trying to get the ambition to start. I think I'm just worried about the transplant. I wish I had someone in my life I could trust to talk to about the upcoming donation, but the only people I have are Scott and Kathleen, and it's not like I can tell either of them how I'm really feeling. I'm scared. There, I said it. Even though my conversations with Dr. Thomas, and all of the ones with Kathleen, solidify in my mind that I'm not only doing the right thing, but I'm the only person who can do it, I'm still terrified of actually going through with the transplant.

I just keep telling myself that this is the right thing for me to do.

So many people are selfish. I see it every single day in the news, and Scott sees it all the time at work. He's constantly telling me about his clients and how willing they are to take advantage of another person. I don't want to be like that, don't want to be willing to screw someone else over just to feel good myself.

But that's exactly what most people do. The world is full of people who want nothing more than to take advantage of others to make themselves feel better and to get ahead. I don't want to be that person. I don't want to be the type of woman people are actually afraid of.

My phone vibrates on the counter, and I snatch it up, turning it quickly so that I can see who is texting. I don't know what I'm expecting, but I shouldn't be surprised when it's Scott.

It'll probably be a long day with Alexander. Don't wait up or make dinner.

Of course. Right when I really want my husband home with me because I'm feeling antsy and a little out of sorts, he won't make it home for dinner. Sighing, I turn and wash the coffee mug I'd set in the sink earlier, then eyeball my phone again.

I know there's one person who will be there for me when I'm feeling so lonely tonight. Part of me wants to reach right out to Kathleen right now, but part of me is nervous.

What would I say? *Hi, I'm just looking for someone to take my mind off things and give me some company tonight?*

Scoffing, I turn away from the sink and dry my hands off. No, that's insane. There's no way I can call her for that. She needs to be there with her daughter and is probably spending time with her mom.

Before I can think too hard about what I'm doing, my fingers are navigating the screen, finding Kathleen's number, and calling it. I feel like I don't have any control over what's happening, and in just a moment, I hear her voice on the other end of the line.

"Hello? Erin?" She sounds sad but also relieved, like she was hoping I would call, but that doesn't make any sense. I'm sure she has plenty of things to do with her daughter right now, but still, the tone in her voice concerns me.

"Kathleen," I say, sounding as bright and happy as possible, "what are you doing?" I don't want to let her know that I'm just looking for someone to make me feel better about myself. The last thing I want is for her to figure out that I'm calling her because I'm lonely.

"Erin, I was . . ." Her voice trails off, and I feel my heart squeeze.

"Kathleen? What happened?"

She's silent, and I think for a moment that she's not going to answer me, but then the words spill out of her like someone pushed over a glass of milk. They sweep over me, and I feel like I'm drowning in them, in their sadness, but all I can do is sit there and listen to what she says.

"My mom died." Three words, all of them so final and painful that I feel each one in my heart. Each word brings me back to the moment in time when my own mother died unexpectedly and I was halfway across the country, trying to put together her funeral.

I remember trying to handle it on my own, not because I

couldn't get help but because I didn't know who to call or what to ask for. Without any siblings, I was all alone, and since my dad had died, there wasn't going to be any help from another parent. Even if he had still been alive, I don't know how much help he would have been.

And as for Scott . . . I love my husband, always have, since the day I walked down the aisle to marry him, but the truth is that I was too afraid to ask him to help me out. He was always so focused on work, so focused on improving himself and doing a better job for his clients that the last thing I wanted to do was bother him.

He would have dropped everything for me, I know that. But I didn't want to be a burden. I remember sitting down on the kitchen floor when I got the call about my mom and sobbing.

I was all alone, and those feelings wash right over me right now when I realize that Kathleen is in the same position.

"I'm coming over," I tell her. "Unless you have someone there with you already who can help you, I'll be there as soon as you tell me where you live." Already, I'm hurrying around the kitchen, grabbing my purse and making sure that my wallet is tucked inside. Kathleen would never ask me to pay for something, but I'm going to be prepared for anything that might come up.

The truth is that death is expensive. And if you have the money, you can make it as noble as possible. If you don't, then your loved one is simply another piece of meat on a slab. I don't know Kathleen's relationship with her mother, but nobody wants to see their mom be treated like that.

"You don't have to," Kathleen finally says. Her voice sounds like she's at the bottom of a deep well. "I'm fine, Erin. Seriously."

"I'm coming." Even if Scott were going to make it home

for dinner, I'd tell him I have something important to do. He'd get it.

She exhales hard. "Are you sure?" When I don't answer, she continues, "225 Richards Street."

"Okay, sit still." I don't want to tell her that I'm coming as much for me as I am for her. I don't want to be alone right now. I know it's silly, but Kathleen is the only person who really understands what I'm going through. "Just sit still, okay? I'll be there in a few minutes. Well, as long as it takes me to get across town."

"Thank you." She sounds exhausted, overwhelmed, and I know immediately that I'm doing the right thing.

"Do I need to bring you anything?" I'm already out the door and in my car. It starts immediately, the engine purring to life, and I back out of the garage, turning the wheel hard to face the car in her direction. "What can I get you?"

"No, nothing." She sounds frustrated and tired, and I get it. I remember feeling the same way when I lost my parents. Only then, I was all alone in dealing with their loss. I'm not going to let her be alone, too.

Kathleen has me. It sounds silly to say, but I'm going to save her life, and that makes her important to me.

I can't help but think that she's going to save mine, too.

32

KATHLEEN

I shouldn't let Erin come here, but it's not like I really gave her permission to. She just hopped in the car and told me she was coming, making any arguments that I had against it die on my lips. It's not that I don't want her here. She was the first person I wanted to call when I found my mom, but that doesn't mean it's a good idea.

I can't go getting close to the person I'm going to have to kill to save me and my daughter.

Cora's on the sofa, her head in my lap. I'm running my fingers through her hair, lifting and dropping the strands before tucking them behind her ear. She shifts, snuggling closer to me, and I lean down to kiss her forehead.

"I can't believe she's gone," Cora whispers. It's the first thing she's said since the police and EMTs left, and her voice is a shock in the still of the house. The only other noises we've heard have been ones from the house settling some on its foundation and even, once, a squirrel running across the roof.

"Me either, darling. It felt like she was going to live forever." I keep my voice as quiet as possible, like doing so is going to honor my mom. But it won't, because she's gone, and she doesn't care how loud we are in the house right now.

I know we were going to leave her behind soon enough anyway, but it still hurts to think about her cold and dead here on the sofa. It's one thing entirely to walk away from her so that Cora and I can have the best possible lives while knowing that she's still healthy and alive, but now she's gone.

It should make it easier, but it makes it harder for some reason.

The sound of a car out front makes me sit up, and even Cora stirs. "Is someone coming?" Her voice sounds hopeful, and I feel terrible that I'm going to get comfort from Erin and she's not.

I'm the only person Cora has. I'm the only one I trust to be near her and get to know her. I have to keep her close to me to make sure she won't question whether or not she really needs a kidney.

The last thing I need is for her to spend a lot of time away from me and for someone to realize that she's not as sick as I say that she is. Keeping her sick ensures that Dr. Thomas will do the transplant, although at this point, I'm not sure that he has any morals.

I found him at the Angry Donkey. That's the basis of every great story, isn't it? Or at least, the ones that are the most messed up. I was there, nursing a glass of whiskey that I definitely shouldn't have been drinking with my kidney already failing me again, after working a hellish shift and making hardly any tips, and he was there next to me, a washed-up doctor who was looking for one last money grab before hanging up his white coat.

One too many drinks led to another, and I learned all about his past history as a surgeon, how he'd fallen from grace after experimental surgeries, how he just needed enough money to move and reinvent himself without anyone ever finding him again.

I told him about my failed kidney, how it was needing to be replaced again, how Cora was showing signs of Alport syndrome. She wasn't, not yet, although I had been keeping an eye on her for any sign that something might happen. I'd warned her of what to watch for, what to tell me about if something terrible happened.

She was healthy. For now.

But why should I make her wait to get sick when there was a simple answer sitting right there next to me at the bar?

I promised him that I could get my hands on some money. I sold everything I could to liquidate my assets and ensure that I could pay him for what he did. Even though I wasn't rich, I had some money from my late husband's estate.

Not a lot, but enough to make Dr. Thomas sit up and take notice. Enough to make him willing to look the other way about where the kidneys for the transplants were going to come from. Enough for him to agree to do the surgeries as long as I could play the part of the desperate patient.

Of course, I would have been the perfect match for Cora. And because the world is cruel, I can't help her by donating my kidney to her. He had to find someone who would be able to donate to us both, and I had to convince her to get on board. And I did.

He found Erin, but I'm the reason she's going to actually have the surgery. We bonded, or at least she thinks we did, and now she'll do whatever she can to help me.

She's kind, too kind, and kindness kills people.

Poor, sweet, loving Erin, who feels so burdened by her wealth and the fact that she wants to do something important with her life that she's willing to walk blindly into a doctor's office to give up her kidneys.

And her life.

There's a wave of guilt that washes over me, but I push it out of the way as I gently lift Cora's head from my lap. "That's Erin," I tell her, still keeping my voice low. "She's coming over to help with Mom. You're welcome to be out here and say hi, but you're also welcome to go to your room, okay?"

"I'm going to my room." She rolls off the sofa, and I watch as she leaves the living room. In a moment, I hear her bedroom door slam, and I turn back to the front door right as Erin knocks on it.

"Coming," I call. Still, my voice is quiet. I don't need to hold space for my mom. She's dead and not coming back, but I still feel guilty over the fact that I'm alive. This was always the plan, but still, seeing it played out before I was ready for it is strange. I'm uncomfortable, and I don't even try to put a smile on my face when I open the door.

"Kathleen." Erin sweeps into the house and pulls me to her, wrapping her arms tightly around me. I can barely breathe, she has me snuggled so tightly up against her, but after a moment, I relax. "You poor thing. That had to be a terrible shock this morning. What can I do for you?"

"You're doing it," I finally manage to say. "Seriously, Erin, you're doing it." My voice breaks, and I feel the tears slide down my cheeks. There's no way I can move to try to wipe them away. All I can do is lean against this woman and let my tears soak into her shirt.

I want to call her my friend. I want to tell her everything that's going on, but if I do that, she'll leave. She'll turn her back on me, and on my daughter, and I can't let that happen. I've found a great friend for the first time in my life, someone who I think will stand by me no matter what, but it's too late.

The one person I consider my friend is the only person who can save my life. And Cora's.

If I tell her the plan, she'll leave. She'll call the police; she'll have me locked up. I can try to keep her as my friend for as long as possible, but it's all going to fall apart eventually.

Either she's my friend and only saves me with one kidney, or I save my daughter.

I've never had a friend like this before. I guess I'll have to enjoy it for as long as possible.

33

My heart breaks when I see Kathleen's house. I feel terrible that she lives here, trying to survive while she's so sick, and I'm right across town in a home that looks like it could be in a magazine. Coming from my gorgeous home, where you could eat off the floor if you wanted to, to here, where you have to be careful where you sit down because there are stains on all of the furniture, is a huge shock.

Still, I'm here for her, not for me. It doesn't matter what her house looks like. She's kind, she works hard to take care of her daughter and volunteer, and I want to help her.

Other people might judge her for the condition of her house, but I just want to be here to support her.

Those are the thoughts running through my head as I walk through the front door. I feel my heels sinking into the dirty carpet and pull back from Kathleen's hug long enough to take her by the hand.

"Come outside and get some fresh air," I tell her, leading her to a pair of rocking chairs on the porch. "I think that being in the house right now will only make this harder for you. Where's your daughter?"

"In her room." Kathleen sits down and stares across the street. Her feet are planted firmly on the deck like there's no way she's going to rock. I know that feeling—like you're willing to do whatever it takes to ground yourself in the midst of your whole life turning upside down.

"I want to pay for the funeral." My voice sounds loud in the silence of the morning, and Kathleen jerks her head to look at me. Surprise is splashed all over her face, but I'm not going to let her argue with me. "Please, Kathleen. I know how expensive they are, and I know that things are going to be hard over here for you two. Let me help."

She shakes her head. "You're already doing so much. I can't ask you to—"

"You're not asking me. I'm telling you what I'm going to do. Besides, what are friends for?" It feels really good to say that to her, to know that I can help her out. Sure, I'm giving her my kidney, but this is different. I haven't had a girlfriend in a while. I like feeling like we might have a bigger connection with each other than I thought at first.

Why else would I have felt like calling her just when she needed me so badly?

"Thank you." Her voice is quiet, and I reach out to take her hand, giving it a squeeze. Scott doesn't really need me. Yes, he loves it when he comes home and I've got a hot meal on the table and clean clothes in the closet. He loves me and dotes on me, and I have no doubt in my mind that he would do anything I asked him to do.

But he doesn't really *need* me. He loves me. He adores me. He worships the ground I walk on and does everything he can to make sure that I'm happy. But Kathleen?

She needs me. *Really needs me.* Needs me more than simply my donating my kidney to her. I can help her. I can manage everything for her, do the planning for her, and make sure that her mom gets the funeral she would have wanted. It doesn't matter to me that I never met the dead woman. I know her daughter, and that's enough.

Not only do I know her daughter, but I feel a connection to her that I can't deny. We're tied together now in a way not many people would ever understand, but they don't need to.

When you're connected to someone the way that I am to Kathleen, it doesn't matter what other people think.

And when you've fallen on hard times, sometimes you just need someone there to pick you up and dust you off. I can do that for Kathleen, and it sounds like she's going to let me help her out.

"I'll make some calls," I say, dropping her hand to grab my phone. "I know a great funeral director here in town who can set you up with everything you need. We'll make sure that she has a beautiful casket so you don't ever have to think about her someplace uncomfortable. Does that sound good?"

Kathleen nods but doesn't meet my eyes. Empathy washes over me. The poor woman is so overwhelmed that she can barely function right now, but that's why I'm here. I'll handle everything and get her back on track.

"You know what?" I'm ready to call the funeral home, but before I do that, I want to make sure that everything here is taken care of. "I'm going to run to the store and pick up some groceries. I'm sure that you and your daughter won't want to be cooking right now, not with the pain so fresh. Does that sound good? Oh! And we need to write an obituary."

"This all sounds great, but I have one written." Kathleen takes a deep breath and finally meets my eye. "I know that sounds crazy, but Mom wanted to make sure she had a say in how it read. Seriously, Erin, I don't know how I can thank you enough. This is more than anyone has ever done for me."

"It's nothing." I flap my hand at her and nod to myself as I

pull my keys from my pocket. "We'll just put the kidney transplant on hold until we get your mom buried, all right? Does
that sound good to you?"

Her face pales. She already looks sickly, with dark circles
around her eyes, but suddenly, she looks even worse. I eyeball
her, hoping she isn't going to throw up.

"I can't put it on hold," she says, and I hear a tremble in
her voice. "As soon as Dr. Thomas tells me it's a go, we have to
move. You're not going to back out, are you?"

I drop to my knees in front of her. "Listen. When Dr.
Thomas calls, it doesn't matter what we're doing, okay? We're
going to stop everything, drop it all, and go to the hospital.
Do you have someone to look after Cora?"

She nods. "I do." Her voice is so quiet, almost a whisper,
and I lean closer to her to make sure that I can hear her.
"She'll be fine."

"Okay, great." I'm feeling better about this, and I want to
make sure she's on the same page as me. "Don't worry, Kathleen. Even if Dr. Thomas called right now, we'd put everything on hold with your mom, okay? The last thing we want
to do is delay the transplant. I'm here for you."

I hope she believes me. I know that Kathleen needs me,
needs me in a way nobody else does, and I want her to realize
that I'm here for her. We talked about our relationship
changing and growing, and I feel it happening. I'll do
anything for her, including paying for her mom's funeral and
giving her my kidney.

"Great. Thank you." She gives me a nod and sits up like
someone jerked on a rope connected to her spine and pulled
her straight. "As long as you promise me that we'll stop as
soon as we need to for the transplant."

"I'll do whatever it takes to take care of you." Kathleen
needs a win in her life. She's been dealing with more prob-

lems than I can imagine, and it's time for me to take those off her shoulders for a while. "Don't worry, Kathleen," I tell her. "I'd go into surgery right now if that's what needed to happen to take care of you."

34

SCOTT

I'm exhausted after a long day in the courtroom, but I feel like I can't go home until I do a little more digging into Kathleen. I wanted this to be clean, for Erin and myself to walk away from her when it's all over, but my wife thinks the two of them have a connection. I love that Erin has such a kind heart and wants to take care of her, but when I got the text this afternoon while I was in the courtroom that Kathleen's mom died and we were going to foot the bill for the funeral, I got a little worried.

Understandably, I hope.

It's not that I don't want to help this woman. The money is not the issue. It's just that Erin has such a kind heart that she's leaping to do whatever Kathleen needs or wants without really stopping to consider whether it's the right thing to do. I was a little leery when she told me that she and Kathleen were becoming good friends, but that's just who my wife is.

Of course, I didn't want her to become close to the woman, not when we weren't really doing anything to save her life. That was never the plan, but that's my wife, though. She sees the good in everyone. That's just who she is.

I'll just have to be there to pick up the pieces of Erin's heart when Kathleen disappears forever. Dr. Thomas assured me that she'd be gone after the transplant.

I'm struck with the sick feeling that I'm trusting the man too much.

All that matters is that Erin gets through this in one piece.

Never have I met someone so passionate about helping other people. I've never met another person who was that willing to put someone else's needs ahead of their own.

It all started to make sense why she's so giving and kind when she told me about the accident that she was in when she was younger. Had someone not been there to save her, she wouldn't be alive now.

And that's exactly why I want to look into Kathleen. I just want to protect my wife.

From listening to Erin talk about Kathleen and explain her situation to me, it's obvious that the woman is in trouble. It's just that in my career as a defense attorney, I've learned a few things about people.

Like how they're always willing to do whatever it takes to get ahead, even if that means they're going to walk all over you. And how even the nicest people can have something they're hiding.

Not Erin. My wife leaves all her cards on the table. What you see with her is what you get, but I'm not sure about her new friend, Kathleen. I saw the woman in my house, saw the way she adapted to the clothing that Erin bought her. I saw how she adopted the mannerisms of the people she was talking to, even though it was a little obvious to me that she was still nervous and cautious about being invited into our home.

What the hell did I get my wife into by working with Dr. Thomas?

Groaning, I scrub my hand down my face. I'm about to

turn on the computer when Alexander leans into my office. He has a huge grin on his face that I'm sure is a clear sign that he's up to no good. I freeze, my finger on the monitor's power button, and wait for him to speak.

"Drinks? You were on fire in the courtroom today. I think we should celebrate, what do you say?"

I hesitate, wanting to go with him. It would be a lot more fun than what I'm about to do, that's for sure. After a long day in the courtroom and a debriefing that ran well past dinnertime, the very last thing I want to do is fire up the computer and do some online sleuthing, but I feel myself shake my head.

"I have things to do," I tell him, and he cocks an eyebrow at me.

"Things? You know you can't look at porn at work, right?"

"Not that kind of thing." For a moment, I hesitate, wondering if I should come clean with him about what I'm thinking about doing. It's insane, isn't it? To research someone dying of a kidney problem just because they give you a funny feeling?

Then again, I know about funny feelings. I know how they can help me uncover the last bit of evidence that we'll need to get our defendants off scot-free. I know how, if more people listened to their funny feelings, then I'd probably be out of a job.

"You know Kathleen?" I ask, deciding in the moment to talk to Alexander about what's going on. It's a far better option than trying to broach the subject with Erin since she seems to think that Kathleen can do no wrong.

"The kidney lady?" He walks into my office and sits down across from me, draping his long frame into the chair. "Yeah, I know her. We met at your house that one night, remember? What's going on? Erin getting cold feet? Man, I wondered if this entire thing was a mistake." He rolls his eyes. "Why in the world she would agree to just give a kidney to a random person she doesn't know is beyond me. She's a hell of a better person than I am, that's for sure."

"She's better than I am, too." I hesitate, wondering how much I can tell him. If it weren't for the way he's looking at me right now, almost like he can read my mind and see that there's more for me to say, I might brush this all off.

"Something's going on," he breathes, leaning forward and tapping on my desk like he's trying to get the attention of a fish at the aquarium. "I knew it from the moment I met that woman at your dinner party. What is it?"

I shake my head. "I'm not sure. Well, okay, I know that Erin just offered to pay for a funeral. Kathleen's mom died, apparently."

"And you're paying for it?" I nod, and he shakes his head. "Do you even know for sure if she died, or is this just a scam to get some money from you guys? Geez, doesn't she have family or something who can help?"

"She has a twin, but I don't know why they're not helping," I tell him, finally pushing the button to turn on my computer. "Erin has been with Kathleen since the morning, trying to get all of the arrangements set up for the funeral, and I've just been too busy with work to really talk to her."

"Look her up. Or I can call a contact at the police department, but I think that you should be able to find something online by now. When did she die?"

"This morning." My hand trembles as I navigate to the local paper's website. If there's going to be any information about the death, then it'll be here in the obits. "Would it be online already?"

"With Erin running the show? I have no doubt. I know how efficient your wife is when she's planning events or putting together parties. If anyone can get an obit in the paper the same day the person died, then it's your wife."

He's right. When Erin gets an idea about something she wants to do, then she's focused beyond belief. I should know. I've listened in on enough of her phone conversations when she doesn't know that I'm spying to see just how driven my wife is. That's why when I click on the obits link, I'm not surprised to see one from this morning.

Francine Bell.

This is the only obituary from today, so I'm sure it's the right one. I click on the link, then only realize that I'm holding my breath when it's time to read it.

"What does it say?" Alexander hurries around the desk to look over my shoulder. He braces his hand on my chair and leans down, his breath warm on my face. I want to tell him to move, but I'm already reading the obit, my eyes flicking back and forth across the screen as I do.

"*Francine Bell, age 64, went to be with her Heavenly Father this morning. She is survived by her daughter, Kathleen, and granddaughter, Cora.*" I turn to look up at Alexander. "This is her."

Wait. It didn't say anything about Kathleen's twin. Fear grips my throat, and I gasp, my head suddenly pounding.

"Keep going. At least we know for sure that her mom did die this morning. What else does it say?"

"Let me see. *Francine spent much of her adult life battling Alport syndrome as well as heart disease. Although she was not a candidate for a transplant, she fought hard to bring more attention to the disease and to ensure that her daughter would have a long and healthy life following her transplant. This, in addition to the love of her daughter, granddaughter, and friends, is the legacy that she leaves behind.*"

Still nothing about a twin.

"That's weird." Alexander breaks the silence that's growing uncomfortably between the two of us. My heart beats hard in my chest when he speaks. I think he's going to put voice to the thought running through my head, and I'm not sure how I feel about that. "It sounds like Kathleen already had a transplant."

"It does." That's weird enough, but not what I'm focused on right now. I have to work hard to unstick my tongue from the roof of my mouth. I need something to drink, a huge glass of water to be able to speak clearly. Maybe that's why my heart is pounding so hard. Maybe I'm dehydrated.

But I don't think that's it.

Alexander keeps talking like he's totally unaware of the fact that right now, I feel like I can't even breathe. "Did she? Could she have already had a transplant? Why would the obit say that?"

I don't know.

All I know is that if Kathleen already had a transplant and doesn't have a twin, then I clearly don't know all of the details from the good doctor. Who is she, really? And who is the kidney actually coming from? This is why he didn't want to tell me her last name. It's why he didn't want to tell me anything about her that would let me dig into who she really is.

I trusted him to take care of this. I believed him when he told me not to worry. There's only one thing that matters right now, and that's making sure that Erin is okay. I have to get to the bottom of this and figure out all the moving pieces. I trusted Dr. Thomas to take care of my wife, but if he hasn't been telling me the whole story, then I have no idea if Erin is going to come through this in one piece.

My stomach sinks when I realize I have no idea what he's really capable of.

35

Scott calls while I'm at the grocery store picking up a pizza for dinner. Cora still hasn't come out of her room to meet me, but Kathleen told me that's pretty typical for her. I don't have a lot of experience with kids, but from what I've seen with them, teenagers tend to want to spend time on their own as much as possible.

They go from being sweet and wanting to hang out with everyone to dealing with raging hormones that make it almost impossible to talk any sense into them.

I miss his call because there's no way that I'm rude enough to answer the phone while I'm in the checkout line, and I try calling him back a few times before finally checking my messages while I'm already halfway back to Kathleen's. I have no idea why Scott isn't picking up, but he's probably with Alexander.

I push thoughts of my husband from my head and concentrate on my friend. She's been a wreck most of the afternoon, trying to deal with planning the funeral and missing her mom while Cora stayed in her room and refused to come out to help.

Like Kathleen doesn't already have enough to worry about, now she's going to be facing down this major surgery without her mom and while trying to help Cora grieve. It's scary to think about the transplant, but this is what I promised Kathleen I would do for her. At this point, I feel like she needs someone in her life to protect her and look out for her, and that's me. I'm the person who can keep her safe and save her life, and right now, that also involves picking up pizza for her and her daughter.

Still, I'm nervous. I feel like everything is moving faster than I thought it would, and I just keep telling myself that I'm the only one who can help Kathleen. How did Dr. Thomas put it? I'm special. I won't back down.

Scott left a short message, and I play it over the Bluetooth speakers in the car while I drive, shaking my head a little to try to clear it.

"Erin, where are you? I need to talk to you about Kathleen and what you're doing with her. I know it sounds crazy, but I think that she may have already had a transplant. Call me back."

"What in the world?" I've already tried to call him three times to update him on the surgery, and he has to call back when I'm busy. His message makes no sense, and I pull up to a red light and stop, reaching out to tap the button on my phone to call him back, when my phone rings. Kathleen's name appears on the screen, and I bite my lower lip, unsure of what to do before finally answering it.

"I'm on my way," I tell her, scooting forward as soon as the light turns green. "They didn't have fresh pepperoni pizza in the grocery store deli, so I grabbed a cheese one and a pack of pepperoni we can put on it."

"Erin, it's Cora." Kathleen sounds breathless, and I tap the brake without meaning to. Honking behind me tells me that other drivers are not happy with my driving. "She's sick. I

need you here, Erin. I don't know if she's going to be okay."
Her voice breaks, and I feel my stomach twist.

Cora can't be sick. Kathleen can't handle it.

"Kathleen, what's wrong with her?" My palms are sweaty,
but I grip the steering wheel as tightly as possible to keep
from losing control of the car. "Do you need to take her to the
hospital?"

"No," Kathleen says, her voice tight. "I'm taking her to Dr.
Thomas. He can fix this. But I need you. I need you there
with me."

I have to get to the doctor as fast as possible. I don't know
what's wrong with Cora, but I do know that if I'm not there,
Kathleen might not be able to handle it. She needs me, and
I'm not going to let her down, no matter what I have to do. It's
a big thing, to be needed by someone and to know that you're
the only person who can really help them with a problem
they're facing.

"I'm headed in that direction now," I tell her, hanging a
right at the next light. Even though I'm already driving fast, I
press down hard on the gas to encourage my car along. Scott
will want to know where I am when he gets home, especially
if this takes longer than normal, but I don't want to take my
hands off the steering wheel to try to call him.

Besides, his message didn't make any sense. What in the
world does he mean that she may have already had a transplant? That's insane, and it sounds like he's been drinking at
work, which is something I told him he needed to stop. I
know that he and Alexander are good friends, but there's a
huge difference between being good work buddies and
getting sloshed together every single night.

After I made him promise me that he would only drink
with me at the house, it seemed like things took a turn for the
better. He stopped coming home reeking of alcohol, and I

stopped worrying as much. Right now, though, I can't help but wonder if he slipped off the wagon.

Or fell. Or *jumped.*

That's not something I can worry about right now, though. My car eats up the miles to the doctor's office, and I'm already working through what I'm going to say in my mind when I get there. I'll hug Kathleen and tell her how happy I am to be there to help her. I'll tell her that she doesn't have to worry about a thing right now, now that I'm there with her.

She'll be scared, of course, but I'm sure I can calm her down and make her feel better. There's no reason for her to be scared when I'll be there to take care of everything.

She lost her mom, but I'm sure that Dr. Thomas will keep her from losing her daughter on the same day.

My phone rings again right as I pull into the parking lot, but I ignore it. I know it's stupid, but I want to get my arms around Kathleen. I'm so close to her that I just want to be there for her, and as soon as I am, then I'll call Scott. Besides, if he has been drinking with Alexander, then there's no reason for me to think that he'd be able to get here right away or even be coherent on the phone.

There are only two cars in the parking lot, one that I immediately recognize as Kathleen's and another that must belong to Dr. Thomas.

"Funny that it's after hours and there are almost the same number of cars here as there were when the office was open," I murmur to myself. I don't have time to wonder about that, though, so I park my car, throw my door open, and hop out before hurrying up to the main entrance.

The door is locked, and I bang on it. "Kathleen! Dr. Thomas! Let me in!" My voice carries away on the wind, but I'm sure that they're going to hear me knocking on the glass, so I make my hand into a fist and bang again. "It's Erin!"

Kathleen appears in front of me, her eyes wide, her hair flowing out behind her. She skids to a stop on the other side of the door and fumbles with the lock before managing to throw it open. "You came! Thank God!" I'm surprised to see that she's wearing scrubs, but I don't have enough time to really latch onto that fact. It strikes me as weird, but not weird enough to say anything to her about it. Besides, there are other things that are more important to talk about.

Like what's wrong with Cora.

If we're going to be able to help her.

What I can do for her.

I'm about to launch into my questions when she grabs my hand and yanks me into the building. She looks past me, her eyes scanning the parking lot for any other cars.

"Kathleen, is everything okay?"

She's still gripping my fingers but lets go of me long enough to throw the lock on the door before taking hold of them again.

"Is Cora okay? You look so stressed. What can I do?"

"I look stressed?" Kathleen laughs, but there's no humor in it. "Yeah, I'd say that I'm stressed out. My daughter is here, sick as a dog, and I have no idea what's wrong with her."

"And you brought her straight here?" The question is out of my mouth before I can stop it. "Did you call 911?"

"I didn't call 911." She shakes her head firmly. "I didn't want to bother anyone, and besides, I knew that I could count on you and Dr. Thomas. You've been so good to me, Erin, so helpful and honest, and I don't know what I would do without you in my life. Seriously. You're the best. He's got her on an IV, and he said that everything will be okay."

She hugs me, and I stand completely still, letting her pull me close before she releases me and leads me down a hall. It's the same one I've walked down before my appointments with Dr. Thomas, only this time, the lights are mostly off, and there's only one room at the end that's lit up.

Dr. Thomas will be back there with Cora. Hopefully, he'll have everything he needs to take care of her here, but I'm not entirely sure that he will. It's not a hospital, after all. I have no idea if he'll have an entire staff here or will try to take care of Cora on his own.

That doesn't make any sense, though. I turn to Kathleen, about to ask her again why we aren't at a hospital and why there isn't a herd of nurses going in and out of Cora's room to take care of her, but before I can, Dr. Thomas appears at the end of the hall. He has on a white coat and a stethoscope around his neck and is staring at the two of us like he's thrilled that we just arrived for the party.

As far as I know, though, there isn't any party here. There isn't any reason he should be so happy to see us when Cora is so sick.

I glance at Kathleen, but instead of looking scared, she looks excited.

"Hello, Erin." Dr. Thomas's voice pulls me from my thoughts, and I lock eyes on him. He looks breathless, like a little kid who knows that the present they want for Christmas is under the tree. It's uncanny, how pleased he looks when we both know that there's a girl in the room behind him so sick and in need of medical care. "You're looking good this evening."

I nod at him and grip Kathleen's fingers even tighter. She's still pulling me down the hall, but I'm going willingly. My heart slams in my chest, but not because I'm scared.

I'm so nervous that I can barely breathe. Not for me, because I know that nothing bad will happen to me, but for Cora. And Kathleen. Imagine the fear and terror of losing your parent and having your child fall ill on the same day. I know that I should respond to him, but I can't seem to form any words. My mouth is dry, like I sucked on a lemon, and that makes it impossible for me to speak. Instead, I raise my free hand in greeting.

"She's here." Kathleen is breathless with excitement. "She came, Dr. Thomas. Everything is going to be all right."

Wait, what? I came to be here for Kathleen, but that doesn't mean I can be of any help. What in the world is she talking about? My heart picks up the pace, and I feel my palms grow sweaty. Even though there's a voice in the back of my head screaming at me to stop moving and figure out what's going on, I keep walking toward Dr. Thomas like I'm on autopilot.

"Everything will be fine." Dr. Thomas smiles at the two of us. "Erin," he says, turning his attention to me, "we're going to move on the transplant tonight. We've got to do this now, before Kathleen gets sicker." Dr. Thomas steps to the side and sweeps his hand open for us to walk into the back room.

I stop dead in my tracks. "But *Cora* is sick," I argue. Kathleen is still holding onto me so tightly that I can't pull away from her. "Why would we do the transplant now when Cora is the one who is so sick?"

"We don't have a choice," Dr. Thomas tells me, his voice soothing. "It's now or never, Erin."

I'm so confused, but I don't want to admit that to the two of them. I trust Dr. Thomas, and Kathleen and I are friends, but I don't see why we have to do this tonight. Not when Cora is so sick. Not when Kathleen just lost her mom.

Shaking my head, I back up from the two of them. I want to call Scott. I want to stop in the middle of the hall here and try to figure this all out until it actually makes sense, but I can't. All I can do is keep walking. I've always done everything I can for other people, and now it's like I can't break out of that.

Dr. Thomas is still to the side of the door, his arm open to gesture us in. Something isn't right, but I turn the corner into the room anyway. My body is on autopilot even though there's a voice in the back of my head screaming at me to get out of here.

But I don't run. I can't, not when I promised Kathleen I would help her. Besides, Scott's the one who found Dr. Thomas to be my doctor, and I know that my husband wouldn't ever let anything happen to me.

Taking a deep breath, I turn into the room. I know what I'm going to find in there. I'm going to find two operating tables, one of them ready for me. I'm going to find one anesthesiologist, willing and ready to do what needs to be done so that nobody wakes up during their surgery. That's the plan. Why it's happening right now, I'm not entirely sure, but apparently, we need to move. Who am I to tell Kathleen that I'm going to back out? Who am I to tell her that we need to wait a little longer?

I can't do it. *I just can't, and I won't.* I promised her that I would help, that I'd be there for her, and I don't have a choice. *It's the right thing to do.*

But before I can walk through the door, someone starts yanking on the front door to the office, the slamming and pounding of the door shaking in its frame reverberating throughout the entire building.

I turn to look behind me, but not before I see that there are three operating tables in the room.

36

SCOTT

"Erin!" My voice is raw already from screaming for my wife, but I'm not going to turn around and walk away from this until I know that she is safe. She's here, I know she is. The little tracker on her phone led me right to this parking lot. I wasn't sure where she would be, so I checked her location before getting in my car and following her here. Why Dr. Thomas is performing the transplant at his office and not at the hospital was beyond me until I remembered that he lost all hospital privileges years ago.

Erin and I must have kept calling each other at the same time to keep missing each other like we were. When Dr. Thomas called and told me that he needed to do the transplant tonight, I freaked out. I have no idea who he's getting the kidney from since, apparently, Kathleen doesn't have a twin.

I have to find out what he's really up to. I promised her that I'd be here for her when she went through the transplant, but more than that, I'm worried about what he's going to do.

He lied. He lied about the twin and where he was getting

my wife's kidney, so what else has he lied about? Grabbing the door handles, I yank hard on them, but the doors are locked and only rattle in place. I shake them, slamming them back and forth like I'm going to be able to burst through to find my wife.

After I helped keep him out of jail a few years ago, I've been keeping tabs on him. Medical malpractice is no joke, but I took the case on and fought for him. Part of me felt bad for the family suing him over the loss of their loved one, but they didn't just die on the table from an accident or negligence.

I know the truth. I found out that Dr. Thomas actually harvested organs from his patient and gave them to someone else. He's been doing this for years, amassing enough money to pay for the women he likes to spend time with and hoping to one day retire. My payment is the final amount that he needs to pay off his debts and live the life he's always wanted.

He's been operating out of this office on the down-low, keeping quiet, making sure that nobody knows who he really is.

But I know.

I know everything.

Or I did until now.

I'm about to start screaming for my wife again when Dr. Thomas appears on the other side of the door. He's angry, his face dark, his eyes brewing storms that make him look evil. "Could you cause less of a scene? I'm going to take care of all of this tonight, but you're going to scare them." He spits the words at me, and I'm actually surprised by his anger. He shouldn't be mad at me. I'm the one who's going to bankroll this transplant.

I'm the one who is going to make sure that he can live out the rest of his days in the lap of luxury.

"Kathleen already had a transplant and doesn't have a

twin, so who the hell is Erin getting a kidney from?" I spit the words at him. "You lied to me about who you're getting the kidney from! You'd better not be giving my wife a bad kidney that will only end up making her sicker. I swear to God, Thomas, that I'll kill you if you hurt my wife."

"You really think that threatening me right now is a good idea?" Dr. Thomas hisses at me, unlocking the door and opening it just enough for him to whisper through the crack at me. "You think that I would give Erin a bad kidney when there's so much money riding on this transplant? Give me some credit, Scott! Remember which one of us really needs me to do this! I want your money, but it's your wife's life on the line."

I've paid this man too much money already just to give him any more credit without getting any answers. I know that if he really has a good plan in place, I should walk away and let him take care of it, but I can't seem to move. My feet feel stuck to the sidewalk outside the building. Wind whips around us, making me shiver, but I'm not willing to leave.

Not until I have all the answers and not until I know that my wife is going to walk away from this.

"So what's the plan, Dr. Thomas? Who the hell are you getting the organ from? I've been trusting you to take care of Erin, and you lied to me, but know this—I will kill you. I'll expose you. I'll grind you into the dirt, Thomas. Just you wait."

"Keep your voice down. I told you that she was the perfect match for Kathleen and her nonexistent twin, but she's also the perfect match for someone else. That's the donor, Scott." He glances over his shoulder.

I can see a light at the far end of the hall. There should be an entire team in there to help him with the surgery, but they didn't park in the main parking lot, which tells me that they're around back, just waiting on him to call them to him.

Why they're not there now, I'm not sure, but I'm tired of waiting around to find out.

"Who? Tell me. Who the hell is the actual donor if it's not Kathleen's twin, and why the hell should I trust you?"

I shove the door forward, causing him to take a step back in order to catch his balance. He scowls at me. "It's Kathleen's kid."

"A kid?" A wave of nausea washes over me. "How old is she?"

He shrugs. "Does it matter?" He sneers the question at me before laughing. "This . . . your face? That's why I never wanted to tell you. How willing are you to do what needs to be done to save your wife, Scott? You wanted a kidney for your wife, and I found you one. You should be grateful that I've even entertained this little idea of yours as long as I have and didn't go straight to the cops. I'm sure that they'd love to know how you're taking a kidney for your wife from someone who thinks they're getting hers!"

His voice is louder now, but nobody comes down the hall to check on us. I'm nervous, dancing back and forth a little outside the building. In the courtroom, I know exactly what to do. I always know what to do with Erin thanks to the cameras and trackers that I have set up. She can't pick her nose in the fog without my knowing that she's done it, and I like that.

I like being in control.

But Dr. Thomas isn't playing by the rules.

He made new ones, and I had no idea that the game had changed. Now he has a kid involved, and the very thought of a kid getting hurt is enough to make me sick. I'm going through all of this so that I can make Erin perfect and healthy before we have kids. He guessed that I wouldn't agree if I knew the truth.

"I need to be a part of this," I tell him. "You let me in. Now. Or it's all off."

"And your wife dies?" He chuckles and shakes his head. "No, Scott, if you want sweet Erin to walk away from this with a kidney, then you need to sit down and shut the fuck up. I've got this under control. Your wife is more than ready to go under the knife for me. We're not going to stop this now. Besides, you don't want that, do you? How do you think Erin would feel if she found out the truth? Trust me, she's ready for this."

He's right and I know it. My stomach sinks. Erin is so innocent and trusting. She'll never question getting on that operating table and letting Dr. Thomas cut her open. I know that I don't have a way to stop this from happening right now, and what's worse, so does he.

If I shove my way into the building and call out to Erin, then the entire thing will be off. Kathleen will know that we've been one step ahead of her this entire time. She'll figure it out. She'll run. The daughter will go with her, and so will our hope of getting Erin a kidney.

Or I can do what the doctor is telling me to do and shut up. I can stay outside, waiting on any news, and hope that he's able to control not only Kathleen and Erin, but also this kid. A sense of dread washes over me when I think about the fact that he's taking a kidney from Kathleen's daughter to save my wife, but he has to.

But the kid will be fine. She can live with one kidney, just like my sweet Erin was going to do for Kathleen.

"Fine," I say, releasing my pressure on the door. A grin spreads across Dr. Thomas's face, and I want to hit him to wipe it off, but instead I take a deep breath and a step back. "Have her call me from your phone before you put her under, do you understand?"

"You don't have to worry about a thing, and you don't get

to tell me what to do." He shuts the door and snaps the dead-
bolt into place, the sound so final that my eyes flick away
from his face to look at the lock. "Trust me, Scott. I wouldn't
do a thing to hurt your sweet wife. She'll walk away from this
in one piece, I can promise you that."

I want to believe him. I do. But before I can feel at all
comforted by his words, there's a scream from down the hall.

Erin.

37

KATHLEEN

"Why are there three beds?" Erin asks. "We should only need two. Why isn't Cora in her own room?"

My daughter is stretched out on the third, so exhausted from what I've been giving her to make her sick that she's completely passed out, and I watch as Erin glances at her before turning back to look at me.

Her eyes are wide, and her voice is high as she stumbles away from me across the room. It's stupid that she would be so upset, suddenly so aware of what's happening to her when she's normally so blind to what's going on around her and caught up in her own mind that she missed all the signs of what's about to happen.

"That's just the setup of the room, and it lets him keep an eye on Cora," I tell her, holding my hands out in front of me and advancing toward her. I try to keep my voice quiet and low so she won't scream again. The last thing we need is for someone to be out for a late walk and to hear her. If they called the police, or if Scott showed up, then this would all come crashing down around us, and I can't let that happen.

I wasn't joking when I told Erin that Cora was sick today. I pushed my daughter too hard—gave her more of the drug and alcohol to calm her down after Erin left.

She was inconsolable, screaming and throwing things, and I offered her a drink to help her chill out. I had no idea that it would be too much, that it would push her over the edge. We have to save her, and that's why I brought her here.

Dr. Thomas told me to get her here immediately so that he could pump her stomach and start an IV and that I needed to figure out how to get Erin here, as well.

I wasn't pretending when I called Erin, freaking out about Cora. Dr. Thomas promised me that he'd take care of her, but he told me that we needed to move on the transplant, that he wanted to do it tonight, when Cora was already in his care and wouldn't question anything. He told me that he was ready to leave the country, and that meant that I needed to get Erin here.

That was the easy part.

Now, the only thing that matters is getting Erin to calm the hell down.

"Listen, Erin," I say, stopping on one side of an operating table. She's on the other, her hands planted on it, staring at me like she can't believe what's happening. Her eyes are so wide that I can see the whites all the way around the pupils, and I roll my neck, cracking the vertebrae as I try to think through how to calm her down. "You really need to calm down. You promised me that you'd help me no matter what, remember?"

"You." She points at me, her finger trembling a little bit in the air. "You're up to something, I know it. You can try to hide it all you want, but why would you bring me to an operating room instead of the hospital? Or a doctor's office? Is Cora even sick?" She eyeballs my daughter. "You know what?" Her hands flap down to her sides like she's trying to fly. "I'm done.

I'm calling Scott and leaving. This isn't right. There's just no way that this is right, I'm sure of it."

I watch as she pats her pockets for her phone, but I'm not surprised when she comes up empty. Someone like Erin, so willing to leap to action to save someone else when they need help, isn't necessarily going to be thinking straight when it comes to taking care of herself.

"You leave it in the car?" I ask, and she grits her teeth as she stares at me before speaking.

"I'm going to walk out that door," she tells me, pointing to the one that we came in together. "And you're going to let me go. I don't know what the hell this is, but I don't like it, and you can't stop me. You can't keep me here."

"Oh, but you see," I say, stepping to the side so that I can stop her from getting past me, "that simply can't happen." We're in a standoff around the first bed.

She looks terrible, but all I wanted to do was make her just sick enough that Dr. Thomas would be willing to perform the surgery on her. It made me feel better to bring her to him with symptoms that could easily be explained away by needing a new kidney.

This is my fault that she's so sick, but I push that thought from my mind. I'm also the reason my daughter is going to be healthier than ever, and I refuse to feel guilty about what I've done to save her.

Of course, now that I think about it, I don't think that he would have told me no even if she'd come into his office doing cartwheels. The man is money hungry, and as long as I was willing to pay, he was willing to look the other way. He didn't care that I'd already had a transplant. He didn't care that Cora didn't really need one.

And he didn't seem to care one bit that Erin was going to end up dead so that the two of us could live.

"What's your plan?" She spits the words at me. "You're

going to take my kidney for yourself and then . . . what? Why is Cora here?" There's pain splashed across her face. "Is she really sick? Is this about money? I would have given you the money," she says, her voice thick with anguish. "I would have given you whatever you needed. All you had to do was ask."

"I know. You're too good, too kind," I tell her. My voice is sharp, and I know it, but I can't help it. I like her, I really do, but I can't like her if I'm going to be able to go through with this. I can't have both her kidneys and her friendship, and I just need to make sure that she's still on board right now. I see the look of fear on her face, but she can't back out now. "You have everything, you know that? And I have nothing. I don't want your money, Erin, but you can still help me. Please! You have to help me."

Her face is pale, like I just slapped her. "Kathleen, I'll help you, but I don't get it. Why is Cora here and not in the hospital? Why do we have to do it tonight? It doesn't make any sense! I want to wait. I want Scott—" she says, but Dr. Thomas interrupts her.

"Is everything all right in here?" His voice is low and calm. He's behind me, and I can't see him, but I don't need to turn around to look at the man who is on my side. He'll shut this down. He'll make sure that Erin stays as pliable and giving as she has been this entire time, and then I won't have to worry about Cora or about me.

"No!" Erin's voice is loud and tight, and she sounds horrified. "You care to tell me what's going on? Kathleen told me that Cora was sick, and I came here to help her out, and you said we have to do the transplant tonight, but I don't get it!" She shakes her head before reaching up and rubbing her temples. "Why will Cora be in here while we're doing the transplant? Why are there three beds?"

"Erin." Dr. Thomas walks slowly toward her. I see the syringe he has held in his hand, but I don't think that she does. His arm is angled away from her so that she won't be able to see the flash of the needle before it's too late. "This is just the best place to bring Cora so that I could take a look at her and still make sure that Kathleen gets her kidney. Nothing is going on."

Erin's eyes flick back and forth between the two of us, and I think that I actually see her relax a little bit, but then she stiffens again and shakes her head. "I want to get my phone and call Scott. I need to let him know that I'm here and what's going on. None of this makes any sense."

"Of course." Dr. Thomas stops walking toward her and swings his arm out to the door. "Go on. Get your phone, call your husband, and then you can come back and be with Kathleen. I'll start taking care of Cora while you're gone."

I lick my lips. My mouth feels suddenly drier than I can handle, and I know it's only because I'm nervous right now that Erin is really going to leave the room. Still, I don't say anything as she slowly walks past Dr. Thomas toward the door. Right as she's about to pass him, his arm flashes out, and I watch as he sinks the needle into her arm.

"Ow!" Erin cries out and spins toward him, but not before he depresses the plunger.

"Kathleen! Help me!" His voice is loud, and I suddenly feel like my body has broken out of ice. I can move again, and I hurry toward the two of them, grabbing Erin around the waist as she loses her balance.

"What the hell was that?" Erin's voice already sounds weak, and I suddenly want to know the answer, too. What in the world could you give someone to make them instantly start to pass out like that?

"Just something to help you relax. You're too high-strung, Erin. You need to calm down." He looks at me as he helps her slump against his body. "We need to get her to an operating table. Lift her feet. Go slow. The last thing we want to do is drop her."

I'm not sure why it would really matter if we dropped her since she's not going to wake up from this, but I don't mention that. The full gravity of what we're doing has hit me, and I'm sure that Dr. Thomas is feeling it, too. The last thing I want to do is make him second-guess what he's doing here.

He has to save me. And Cora.

Still, a pang of regret shoots through me when we get Erin settled on the table. She looks so peaceful, like she's taking the world's best nap, and I brush her hair back from her face so that I can get a better look at her. Her eyelids don't flutter; she doesn't twitch under my touch, nothing.

"Let me get her hooked up, and then we'll get you ready, okay?" Dr. Thomas doesn't look at me while he speaks. Instead, he hurries around Erin's body, moving quickly as he starts an IV. Even though I know what we're doing, the sight of blood still makes me a little squeamish, and I look away from the red that rushes from her body to fill the first inches of tubing before the saline can stop it.

"What happens now? Are we sure that tonight is the right time to do this? What about Cora?" I'm surprised at how strong my voice sounds. I'm terrified right now, not because of what's going to happen to Erin but what's going to happen to Cora. I look over at my baby, taking in the tube that already runs to her arm. She looks so small there on the operating table.

This surgery is a big deal. She'll feel terrible when she wakes up. We'll both have a long road to recovery, but I already have a hospital halfway across the world ready for us. We'll travel as soon as we can and be taken care of there. It's all planned out.

"Yes, what about Cora?" He pins me in place with his

stare. "Care to tell me exactly what you gave her to make her so sick?"

I freeze. "How the hell do you—"

"I'm not an idiot, Kathleen. I know that you've been making her sick. Now I just have to pray that she's not too sick to do the transplant."

Did I push it too far? I'll never forgive myself if I'm the reason my daughter can't get the kidney that she needs in the end. "What do I need to do?"

"You just need to get up on the last table and let me do my thing." His words are clipped. I can tell that he's in the zone, so I don't argue with him. "I'll get your IV started and then call in the rest of my staff so that we can get started on the transplant."

"Transplants," I correct him, climbing onto the operating table. Excitement rushes through me as he starts an IV. I only have a moment before the medicine is going to hit me and I'm going to pass out. "Transplants. Plural. Right? Dr. Thomas? *Dr. Thomas!*" I blink up at him as I feel myself getting swept under.

But I'm still awake enough to hear him laugh.

"How did it go?" I eyeball Dr. Thomas, trying to read the expression on his face but finding it impossible. He knows how to lie to people and get them to do what he wants, and I don't want him to be able to play me like that. "Is Erin okay? And the girl?"

While I wait for him to answer, I slip Erin's phone into my pocket. It was easy to pick up a burner and then change Kathleen's number in her contacts to be the one to the new phone. I'll never answer the burner, never even turn it on. It'll ring in perpetuity whenever my wife tries to reach Kathleen. The last thing I want is my wife getting in contact with Kathleen when this is all said and done.

"You knew full well that your wife was going to come through this in one piece, Scott. That was the only concern. And I'm surprised that you care about the girl now that Erin has the kidney she needs." There's ice in his voice that I haven't heard there before.

"Of course I care about her," I say, but he cuts me off.

"You know that's why I didn't tell you who the donor really was, right? I knew that you'd do . . . this. Get righteous."

He flicks his wrist at me. "What if you tried to change your mind before the surgery? Not a chance, my friend. I needed everything to go smoothly, or it was all going to fall apart for me. You're all high and mighty about where we got the kidney now, aren't you, but all you cared about before was making sure that Erin came through in one piece. That's why I couldn't tell you. And for your information, the girl is fine. She's young and healthy and will bounce back quickly. Erin will be fine, too. You just have to keep her on these immuno-suppressants for a year."

I take the bottle of pills he hands me and turn it over as I look at them. They're what will keep Erin's body from rejecting the kidney.

The kidney he took from a kid.

I should feel guilty about that, should feel terrible that we took an organ from a perfectly healthy kid and gave it to my wife so that I would feel better about her health, but I don't. I did when I first found out about it, but not anymore. Not when Dr. Thomas is assuring me that both Erin and the kid will be okay.

"She's going to hurt. What do I give her for the pain?"

"These. And these are antibiotics." He hands me more bottles, the pills rattling loudly in them. "She could get an infection and die if you don't make sure that she's on these, do you understand? Don't mess this up, Scott, or it's on you."

"It'll be on you," I tell him, but he just laughs and shakes his head.

"Not a chance. I'm getting the fuck out of here. Thanks to your payment and the money that Kathleen scraped together for me to do the surgeries for her and her daughter, you'll never see me again."

"You don't think that she'll hunt you down?" I stare at him, trying to read his expression. He's not a good man. I've known that since I met him and defended him in court, but it's still a bit of a surprise to know that he's going to willingly walk away from this and let the rest of us deal with the fallout after he's gone.

"Not a chance. She doesn't have the money, for one, and she doesn't have the balls, for another. You have both of those things, but I didn't screw you over, did I?"

I shake my head. "Where will you go?"

"Far away from here." He pats his pocket and then pulls his keys out, jingling them at me. "As far away from here as I can go. Don't look for me, Scott. Have a great life with your wife and whatever kids you decide to have. I want no part in it."

I want to stop him or at least get his attention, but why? There's nothing more that needs to be said between the two of us. We're not friends, never were going to be friends, and the best thing for the two of us to do is part ways and never speak of each other again.

"Be well, Scott," Dr. Thomas says. "Good luck with everything."

"How do I get her home?" I step forward, blocking his path to the door. "She's still here, but how do I get her home? What do I do?"

"Not my problem." He glances at the watch on his wrist, and then his eyes flick up to mine. "But I'd move fast if I were you. You don't want Kathleen waking up first, do you?"

He scoots around me, and I watch him go for a second before shaking my head to clear it and hurrying out of the small office in the opposite direction. Erin's in there. She needs me, and I'm going to do whatever it takes to keep her safe.

I've already proven that I will, haven't I?

39

KATHLEEN

I knew that my body would feel heavy and useless when I woke up from the anesthesia, but it's still uncomfortable. It's been a long time since I last had surgery like this, and I let my eyes flutter shut while I roll my head back and forth on the pillow, trying to get the energy to sit up. My entire body hurts. There's this fluttering in my stomach that tells me I'm going to need to eat something sooner rather than later, but that's not what's really bothering me.

Cora.

Planting my hands flat next to my body on the operating table, I push myself up into a seated position. My head swims, and I close my eyes, clamping them shut as hard as possible to keep from being sick. "Cora," I whisper, my mouth dry.

I lick my lips, hoping that any moisture will help me speak louder than I am right now.

"Cora." Definitely louder, but she still doesn't respond.

Where is Dr. Thomas? Where's the team of nurses who are supposed to be here with us as we both wake up? They should be fawning over me right now, checking my stats, making sure that I'm as comfortable as possible and making sure that I'm not in pain.

That's when I realize that I don't hurt. I lightly touch my side, my fingers dancing across the fabric of my scrubs, then suck in a gasp.

There's no pain.

Now my eyes fly open, and I fight against nausea as I look down at my body. "No," I croak, my fingers working hard to pull the edge of my shirt up. My skin is smooth, unblemished. "No, what did he do?"

No pain. No incision. No bandages.

Fear rockets through me, and I turn, my eyes searching the room for Erin and Cora. The bed next to me is empty, which means Erin's gone, but I can't worry about her right now. I have to find my daughter. An IV runs into the back of my right hand, and I grab the tape, gritting my teeth as I yank it off and slip the needle from my skin.

Swinging my legs over the side of the bed, I force myself to stand up, then pitch forward, grabbing onto Erin's empty bed for support. Cora's on the one next to it, her eyes still closed, her beautiful face so relaxed and at peace that I think for a moment that she's dead.

"Cora!" My voice is stronger now, louder, and I stumble over to my daughter. Her forehead is warm under my touch, and relief floods through me when I realize she's not dead. I trace my fingers down her cheeks, and her eyes flutter, but they don't open.

Turning, I pluck at the edge of her shirt. Her scrubs are the same as mine, but when I tug her shirt up, there are bandages there, bright white and plastered to her body.

"What did he do?" My mind reels as I try to come to grips with what Dr. Thomas must have done to my precious girl. Spinning away from Cora, I search the room for someone to help me. "Where are you?" I scream the words, my throat raw. "What did you do? Get out here!"

Nothing. Only silence presses down on me, so painful that I actually can feel it in my ears. My heart slams hard, panic growing in my stomach, and that's when I see the piece of paper on the floor.

It must have fluttered to the ground when I got up from the operating table I'd been on. I hurry to it, grabbing it in shaking hands, then close my eyes for a moment to calm myself.

There has to be an explanation for all of this. There has to be some reason Dr. Thomas would only be able to save Cora and not me. I need the kidney, but something must have been wrong with one of Erin's. That's why he only operated on my daughter. That's why he didn't do anything to save me.

I read the letter, so cold and cruel in what it says that I find myself sinking down to the floor without realizing what I'm doing.

Kathleen,
It's nothing personal. Erin needed the kidney more than either of you did, and Cora was a perfect match. She'll be fine without two kidneys, although a little sore for a while. I left you a bottle of antibiotics to help her heal, but you will want to see about getting yourself on the transplant list.
Don't try to find me. I'm gone. Don't think that anyone would believe you. If you try to take me down, you're going down with me.

"No," I gasp out, then stand, crumpling the paper in my hand. It's worse than I thought. Not only did he not help me, but he stole from my daughter. He stole life from her. Cold anger washes over me, and I rip the paper, throwing the little pieces to the floor before stomping back over to my daughter.

The effects of the anesthesia have all but worn off now. I'm still feeling a little weak in the knees, but the anger pumping through my veins is enough to keep me going.

"We have to find him," I tell Cora, taking her hand and squeezing it. "And you have to wake up. I can't move you if you're still asleep like this. Wake up, Cora." Tears stream down my face, but I don't bother to wipe them away. "Baby, you've got to wake up."

What if she doesn't? What if the surgery was too much for her? What if I put her under the knife for no good reason, and now she's never going to wake back up?

"Cora." I touch her cheek, then squeeze her hand again, leaning down and getting into her face when I repeat her name. "Cora!"

I can't lose her and my mom. I can't be the reason they're both dead.

She still doesn't move. I don't know if Dr. Thomas is gone already or not, but I can't leave my daughter here. I want to hunt him down and punish him for what he did to the two of us, but he knew me better than I thought. He knew I wouldn't leave her here without making sure that she was okay.

Don't try to find me.

He took all of my money, and probably money from Erin and Scott. He's gone, in the wind, and any chance that I have of hunting him down is getting smaller by the second the longer I stay here with Cora.

But I can't leave her. A sob tears through my body, and I sink down next to the operating table, still holding Cora's hand. I just lost my mom. I lost the kidney that was supposed to keep me alive. I can't lose my daughter.

Dr. Thomas is gone. If he's not now, then he will be by the time Cora wakes up. We have to leave, too. That thought hits me hard, and I stiffen, suddenly listening for anyone who might come by the office. There's no reason staff would come by this late at night or someone would get curious about lights on in the office after hours, but still, my ears prick for any sound.

I have to move her.

"Cora, I'm so sorry," I tell her, unhooking her IV like I'd done to mine just minutes before. The bottle of antibiotics is next to her body, and I grab it. "I'm so sorry." Sobs rack my body, and I can barely pick her up, I'm so upset. She's thin and light, and I tuck her against my chest before stumbling out of the room. "Cora, forgive me," I tell her.

What if Scott sends the police here? He took my daughter's kidney, but what if he tries to hurt me more? It doesn't matter that I don't think Erin would want anything to happen to me. I don't trust her husband.

I don't trust anyone.

I have to leave town. I have to get out of here. With Cora. It's always all been for her.

The first thing I see when I open my eyes is Scott leaning over me, a smile on his face, concern etched between his eyes.

"You're awake," he whispers, reaching out and lightly brushing some hair back from my forehead. I want to lean into his touch, but I can't seem to move. My entire body feels exhausted, like I just ran a marathon and am only now trying to stop and catch my breath.

"I'm awake," I repeat, my voice quiet. "How's Kathleen?"

There's a flash of something on Scott's face. Concern? Worry? I don't know, and it's gone before my fuzzy head can latch onto the expression and try to figure it out.

"She's fine. And Cora is better. They're at Dr. Thomas's office, healing up, but I told him that I wanted to bring you home and let you heal here."

I'm at home. That explains why there's no sharp antiseptic smell and why the bed is so comfortable. "How long was I out?"

"A long time. I just got you back here a little bit ago. Dr. Thomas said that you had to be observed for a while to make sure you didn't run the risk of infection. Still, there's a whole host of pills that you're going to have to take."

"That's fine." I want to sit up, and I reach for him. Scott wraps his arm around my shoulders and carefully helps me up before planting a kiss on the top of my head and stepping back.

"How does it feel?"

"Like someone cut out one of my organs." I groan and lightly run my fingers across where the incision is. I don't need to look at the bandage to know that the surgery was a success. I feel puffy and inflamed, but also really good about what I just did.

I saved her life.

"You were a champ," Scott tells me, grabbing a chair and dragging it over to sit by the bed. I lean back, and he immediately hops up to fluff pillows up behind me.

I knew that surgery would be uncomfortable, but I had no idea how much it would really hurt. I'm sure that I'm on a host of painkillers, but there's a deep tugging and soreness that they can't even touch.

Scott sees the pain on my face. "Oh, darling, you hurt. He told me that you'd need more meds this morning, so let me see what time I can give you some."

While Scott looks through a box of pills that he has on the foot of the bed, I glance around the room for my phone. I want to check in on Kathleen and see how she's feeling. We're more connected now than ever. *I saved her.* There's literally a piece of me in her body, and I feel tears stinging the corners of my eyes at that thought.

"Oh, hey, are you okay?" Scott's by my side in an instant, squeezing my hands and looking into my eyes. "Does it hurt that badly? Erin, what can I do for you?"

I force myself to shake my head. "It hurts, but that's not it," I tell him. "It's just . . . Kathleen and I are so connected now, Scott, do you see that? I want to know if she's okay. I can't believe we did it, that there's part of me in her, keeping her alive."

A sob threatens to choke me, but before I can cry harder, his arms are around me and he's pulling me to him, resting my head on his chest. "You are incredible," he tells me, his hand slowly stroking down my back. "Seriously, Erin, I can't imagine a more amazing person than you."

"I want to talk to her," I say, pulling back from him. "Please, Scott, I need to make sure that she's okay. This is no walk in the park." I let out a little laugh and immediately regret it when pain shoots through my core.

"How about this? You take the pain meds you need before things get too bad, and I'll call her. That way, you can rest, and I can check in on her. How does that sound?"

"You're the best." I take the pills he hands me and pop them in my mouth before taking a sip of the water. He holds the cup for me, carefully tilting it up so I can drink without spilling. "Tell her I'm thinking about her, okay?"

"Will do. You rest. If she's in nearly as much pain as you are, then she might very well be asleep too, right? We don't want to interrupt her from getting the rest that she needs."

He's right. Of course he's right. Scott is always right about everything, which is one of the reasons I'm so glad that I have him.

I don't want to wake her up if she's sleeping. It's just that I think that she might be the best friend I've ever had, and I want to check on her. I want to make sure that she's feeling okay.

I have no idea how long it will take the two of us to recover from surgery, but as soon as we're better, I want to see her. I want to hang out with her, meet Cora. I want to get to know her better.

My eyes are heavy, and I fight to keep them open. I tell

myself that I can sleep after I know for sure how she is, but I'm just so exhausted and suddenly can't stay awake another moment.

THE LAST THING I want to do is tell Scott that I still haven't heard from Kathleen after the transplant. It's been over a week now, and I've called her every single day. Her voicemail was never set up, so I can't leave her messages, but I keep praying that she'll call me back.

Nothing.

It's like she fell off the face of the earth. I remember what she said to me right before the surgery, about how I have everything and she has nothing, but it doesn't have to be like that.

I hear Scott walking into the living room, where I'm perched on the sofa, and I click my phone's screen off and set it to the side, trying to make it look like I wasn't just on it.

But he knows. Somehow, he always knows what I'm doing. It's uncanny, but it has to just be because he loves me so much.

"Still nothing from Kathleen?" Sitting down on the sofa next to me, he wraps his arm around my shoulder and pulls me close. I can lean against him now without any pain or tugging in my side, and I do, relaxing into him and drawing strength from him.

"Nothing." I keep my voice as even as possible even though I want to cry. I thought Kathleen and I were friends. I honestly thought that we'd share this bond now that we'd gone through this together, that we'd stay connected forever.

She was so honest, so real. She's nothing like the wives I tried to be friends with when Scott and I first got married. I never felt like Kathleen was judging me for what I have. She just liked being with me, I'm sure of it, and now I don't get to have that any longer.

"I thought we'd be friends forever," I admit, turning my face into his chest. I'm going to cry, I know it, and I might as well let his shirt soak up my tears. "Why won't she return my calls?"

"Oh, Erin, I don't know." Scott murmurs the words, and I let them wash over me. "I thought that you two really had a connection, but we didn't really know her that well, did we?"

"Why do you say that?" I sit back from him before angrily wiping tears off my cheeks. "What do you mean by that?"

"Just that. I see people at work, Erin, and believe me, not all of them are nearly as good a person as you are. There are tons of people in this world who are willing to take advantage of another person just to get what they want. Kathleen said all the right things and seemed great on paper, but maybe she got the one thing she wanted and then ran."

"No." I shake my head. "No, Scott, you're wrong. There's no way she would have done something like that to me. We were friends." Even as I argue with him, though, I feel doubt growing in the pit of my stomach. What if my husband is right? What if Kathleen really was just taking advantage of me and now wants nothing to do with me?

I don't want to believe it because it hurts far too much.

"I just want you to look at the facts." Scott's voice is still kind, but there's a note of finality to it like he's shutting down the conversation. "And you need to take your vitamins, darling. Why don't you do that, and then I'll make you something to eat?"

"Fine, thanks," I say. My voice is flat, and I know I'm being rude to him, but I can't help it. It's ripping me apart to think that Kathleen would just . . . bail on me like that, but maybe that's exactly what happened. Maybe she really was that kind of person, and I just can't accept it because I wanted to see the good in her.

Scott hands me three pills and a cup of water, then watches while I take them. When I'm finished, he gives me a nod and then takes the cup from me.

"Why so many?" I ask him. "What did Dr. Thomas say about my taking so many?"

"He said that you were really healthy but would need antibiotics for a while to fight off any possible infection, then gave me a vitamin to give you for the next year or so."

"A year?" I frown because that really doesn't make any sense. "Why so long?"

"You were perfectly healthy, Erin, but even healthy people should take vitamins. I'm going to pick up some at the store for me, I think. These are just special ones that are designed specifically for you. I think he did it for you as a way to thank you for being so generous."

"Oh," I say, sitting back on the sofa. It seems a little foolish and rude to not want to take the special vitamins from the doctor, so I guess I'll do it. Scott seems to think it's a good idea, and that gives me peace of mind.

"Don't worry, Erin, you know I'd never do anything that would hurt you, right? I love you so much. I'd do anything to keep you safe and healthy." He looks concerned, and I smile at him.

"I know, Scott. I love you, too."

"That's why I think you need to give Kathleen some time. If she reaches out to you, that's great, but I don't want you to get your heart broken expecting something from her that she's not willing or able to give you."

Here come my tears again, but Scott is right. If Kathleen doesn't want a relationship with me, then I can't force her to have one. She'll reach out to me if she wants to, and if she doesn't . . . well, then at least I know that I did the right thing by her.

That's all I was trying to do. All I wanted was to help her, and I did that, no matter how she acts about it now. We might not be friends like I would have liked, but I saved her life, and that's a pretty incredible thing I've done.

EPILOGUE

It's been almost six years since my mom tried to get me a kidney transplant. Six years since I woke up on an operating table with an incision on my side and missing an organ. Of course, my mom figured out what had happened right away. As soon as she came clean with me about what had happened, I wanted to call the cops, but she didn't.

Dr. Thomas took our money and ran. We never heard from him again except for the note that he left my mom next to her on the operating table. It wished us luck, said that I was perfectly healthy even with just one kidney, and that he couldn't do what she wanted. It also said that if she tried to find him, he would take her down with him.

She said that we had no recourse, but I think she was just scared of what would happen to me if she hunted him down. Everything had been done in secret, and there wasn't any proof. More than that, she said that there was no way any cops would believe her over Scott and Erin Anders. No way that they would believe that Dr. Thomas took my kidney, gave it to Erin, then left both me and my mom on the operating tables until we woke up.

And maybe she was right. We'll never know now, though, because she died two years ago, and I've been trying to find my way in the world without her. At first, I didn't want to come back to the town where we lived with my grandmother. As soon as I was okay to travel, Mom had put me in the car and we'd driven away. She'd promised me that everything was going to be okay. We moved to Atlanta, a big enough city where we could blend in and one with enough bars for my mom to work multiple shifts while I finished school. We were poor. Poorer than we'd been before after giving Dr. Thomas everything, and the two of us took advantage of every social program we could to get help.

I didn't love Atlanta, but it was better than being somewhere where I'd have to deal with all the memories of my grandmother dying in the house. Still, after my mom died, I knew what I had to do. I'd promised her that I'd never forget her, and that meant I needed to return home. This place is loaded with memories, and I was sure that just being here would upset me, but it hasn't.

It's probably been good for me, if I'm being honest. Not only was I able to sell the property to the city, who wanted to tear down the abandoned house and put up a parking lot, but with that money, I was able to afford a small condo by myself. I live there with Frank, my dog, and mostly keep to myself.

Except when I'm at work, which is where I am now. Even when I was younger, I knew that I wanted to work with kids when I grew up. I love teaching them and seeing the lightbulbs in their heads go off when they finally understand something. That's why I'm in school to get my degree in early childhood education. Thankfully for me, after two semesters of classes, I was able to get a job teaching at a preschool in the morning.

Night classes are hard, but I'm willing to put in the work.

I'm going to do whatever it takes not only to live my dream, but also to honor the memory of my poor mom.

"What do you think about your room, sweetheart?" The woman's voice pulls me from my thoughts and makes me look up. I've heard it before, although only through the walls at my house when I was little, but I always knew that I wouldn't forget it. Erin stands in the door to the classroom, tightly holding her daughter's hand as they survey the brightly lit pre-k room. There are small cubbies along one wall of the room and tables with tiny little chairs in the middle of the room. In one corner is the circle time rug and a bookcase packed with books for the kids to read. There are toys and even a little bathroom for the kids to use.

Rose. Her daughter's name is Rose. I know that from the information sheet that her parents had to fill out when they registered here at the preschool. Because of that, I also know that her favorite color is blue, she likes horses, and she wants to be a doctor when she grows up. In the little section where parents can write notes about their kids that may help us better understand family dynamics, her mom wrote that they'd been wanting children for a while and were finally blessed with Rose.

Blessed.

"I like the room." Rose gives a firm nod as she looks around the room. "It'll be fun."

"It sure will." Leaning down, Scott gives her a kiss on the top of her forehead, then stands up and walks over to me to introduce himself. "Rose's dad," he says. "Scott Anders."

"Miss Anne," I say, reaching out to shake his hand. "I'll be working with Miss Jackie. This is my first year here, but I think we're going to have a lot of fun."

He nods and then leans forward to speak quietly to me. "Listen, I talked to Miss Jackie about this already, but I think this separation is going to be harder for my wife than it is for

Rose. She went through a pretty rough time emotionally shortly before Rose was born. If you could just let us know right away if there are any problems or concerns with Rose's behavior or separation anxiety, we'll take care of it right away."

I keep my voice just as quiet. "Not a problem. We'll keep a close eye on Rose and make sure that she's always safe. Trust me, Mr. Anders, she's in the best hands here."

Before he can say anything else, Rose walks up to me and points to a small tattoo on my wrist. "What's that for?"

"I got this to remember my mom," I tell her, keeping my head down so that I don't have to make eye contact with Erin, who is now crossing the room to talk to me too. "I lost her two years ago, and having how she signed '*Love, Mom*' here makes me feel closer to her."

I'm pretty sure that Erin won't recognize me. Mom said that Erin only saw me once, when we were supposed to have the kidney transplant, but I was much younger then, and Erin was so stressed out about what was going on that she didn't think she'd remember anything from that night. Still, I don't want to risk it by looking her straight in the face.

It's also why I changed my name to my mom's middle name. Sure, I loved my name, and I still do, but I want to honor my mom, and I want to get close enough to Erin and Scott without them figuring out what I'm going to do.

After we ran, my mom ended up explaining everything to me. She confessed how she was afraid that I would need a transplant and how she made me sick so that I wouldn't argue with her when she took me to the doctor all the time. I'd been horrified at first, of course, and even thought about running away, but she begged me to stay.

She begged me to try to see it from her point of view, to see how hard she'd tried to keep me safe. It wasn't her fault that she had to make me sick, she told me. She only did it so that I wouldn't rebel and fight her when she tried to take care of me. She explained it all, explained the drug she gave me to make me sick, explained how it made me feel.

She told me that she was the only person who loved me enough to do whatever she had to do to keep me healthy. A lot of people say that they'll do whatever it takes to save someone, but she was the only person who loved me enough to actually go through with what it took.

I know everything. I know how she tried so hard to save me and what she was willing to do to protect me. In the end, I was the healthy one, even without my second kidney, and she died. It isn't fair that I don't have her. It isn't fair that she couldn't get a healthy kidney and that Scott and Dr. Thomas were working together.

Rose speaks to me and pulls me out of my thoughts. "I asked if we have a snack every day."

"We sure do." I plaster a smile on my face. "Starting tomorrow on your first day. And let me tell you a little secret, Rose. Miss Jackie is terrible at opening fruit cups, but I'm great at it. Just let me know if you need help with anything."

"Oh, that's a relief," Scott interjects, and I look at him. "It's such a nightmare opening those things without making a mess."

"Not a problem," I tell him, then slip my hand into my pocket and finger the small vial there. Even though I knew we weren't going to have a snack today, I wanted to bring it with me just to make sure that I could carry it without someone seeing it. It won't be a problem to open her fruit cups, and it certainly won't be a problem to give her what my mom gave me.

Nobody will see me put drops of it in her snack. Rose certainly won't be paying enough attention to say anything to stop me. Nobody will know why she's suddenly so sick, why she feels awful but her symptoms can't be explained with a simple diagnosis.

My mom begged me to remember her, and I will. She knew the fear of a parent who wants to save their child and will do anything to keep them safe, and soon Erin and Scott will, too.

THANK YOU FOR READING

Did you enjoy reading *The Promise*? Please consider leaving a review on Amazon. Your review will help other readers to discover the novel.

ABOUT THE AUTHOR

Emily Shiner always dreamed of becoming an author but first served her time as a banker and a teacher. After a lifetime of devouring stacks of thrillers, she decided to try her hand at writing them herself. Now she gets to live out her dream of writing novels and sharing her stories with people around the world. She lives in the Appalachian Mountains and loves hiking with her husband, daughter, and their two dogs.

ALSO BY EMILY SHINER

The Secret Wife

The Promise

Made in the USA
Columbia, SC
17 February 2022

56370040R00162